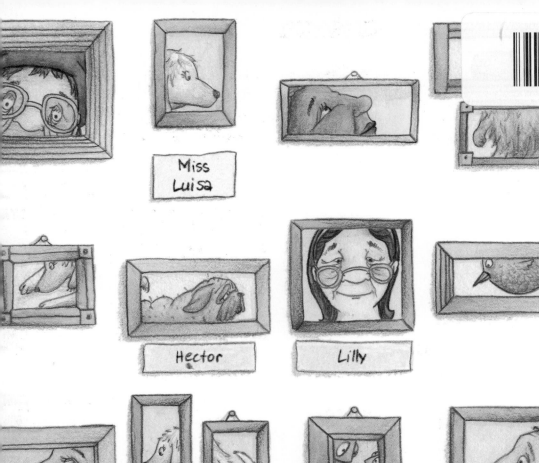

Miss
Luisa

Hector

Lilly

Harry

Agatha

A giant thank you to the many children who helped me uncover the secret life of little old ladies. With an inquiry on the topics "to be old, to become old, and old people" four- to ten-year-olds explained to me, among other things, how it feels to be old, what old people do all day long, where their strengths and weaknesses lie, and naturally how to imagine little old ladies. F. K.

minedition
published by Penguin Young Readers Group

Illustrations and text copyright © 2008 by Franziska Kalch
Original title: Alte Damen
English text adaption by Kathryn Bishop.
Coproduction with Michael Neugebauer Publishing Ltd., Hong Kong.
Rights arranged with "minedition" Rights and Licensing AG, Zurich, Switzerland.

Published simultaneously in Canada.
Manufactured in China by Wide World Ltd.
Typesetting in Optima by Hermann Zapf.
Color separation by the artist.

Library of Congress Cataloging-in-Publication Data available upon request.

ISBN 978-0-698-40087-0
10 9 8 7 6 5 4 3 2 1
First Impression

For more information please visit our website: www.minedition.com

Franziska Kalch

Little Old Ladies

Translated by Kathryn Bishop

minedition

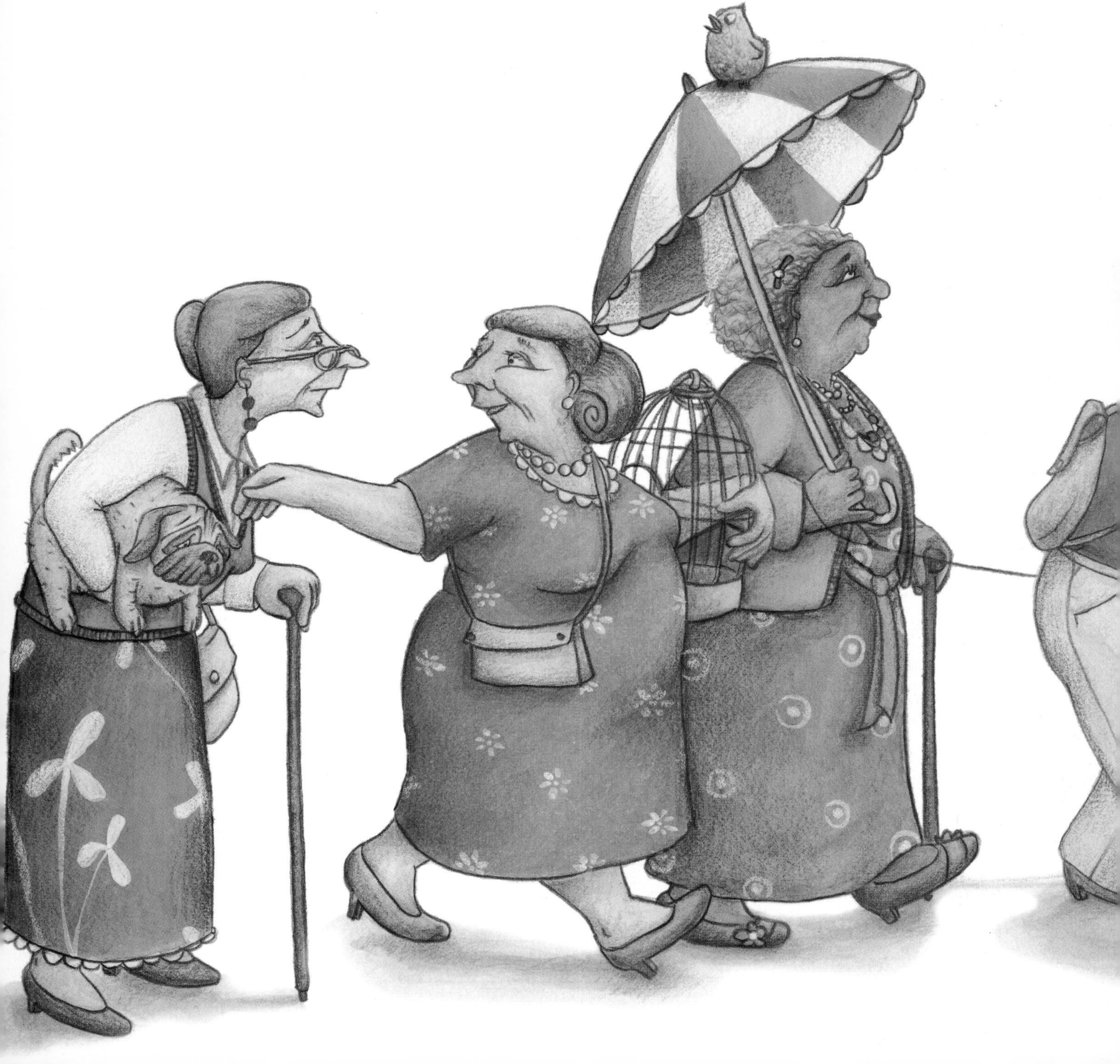

If you think little old ladies just sit around all day feeding
the ducks in the park, you are mistaken.
Their lives are really quite different.

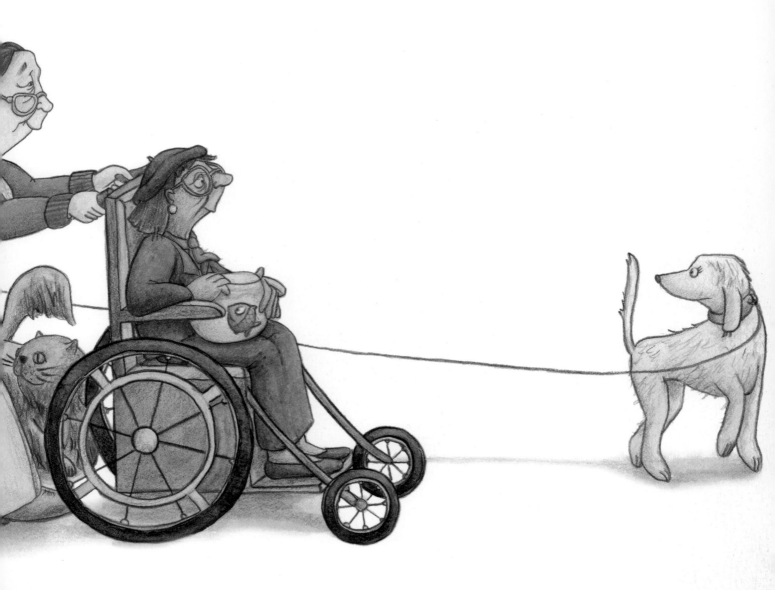

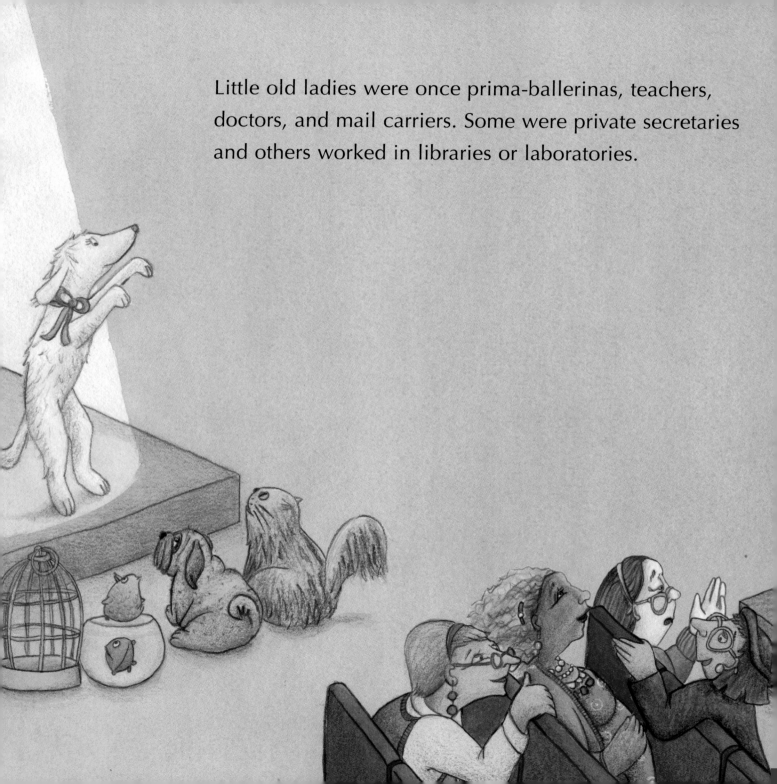

Little old ladies were once prima-ballerinas, teachers, doctors, and mail carriers. Some were private secretaries and others worked in libraries or laboratories.

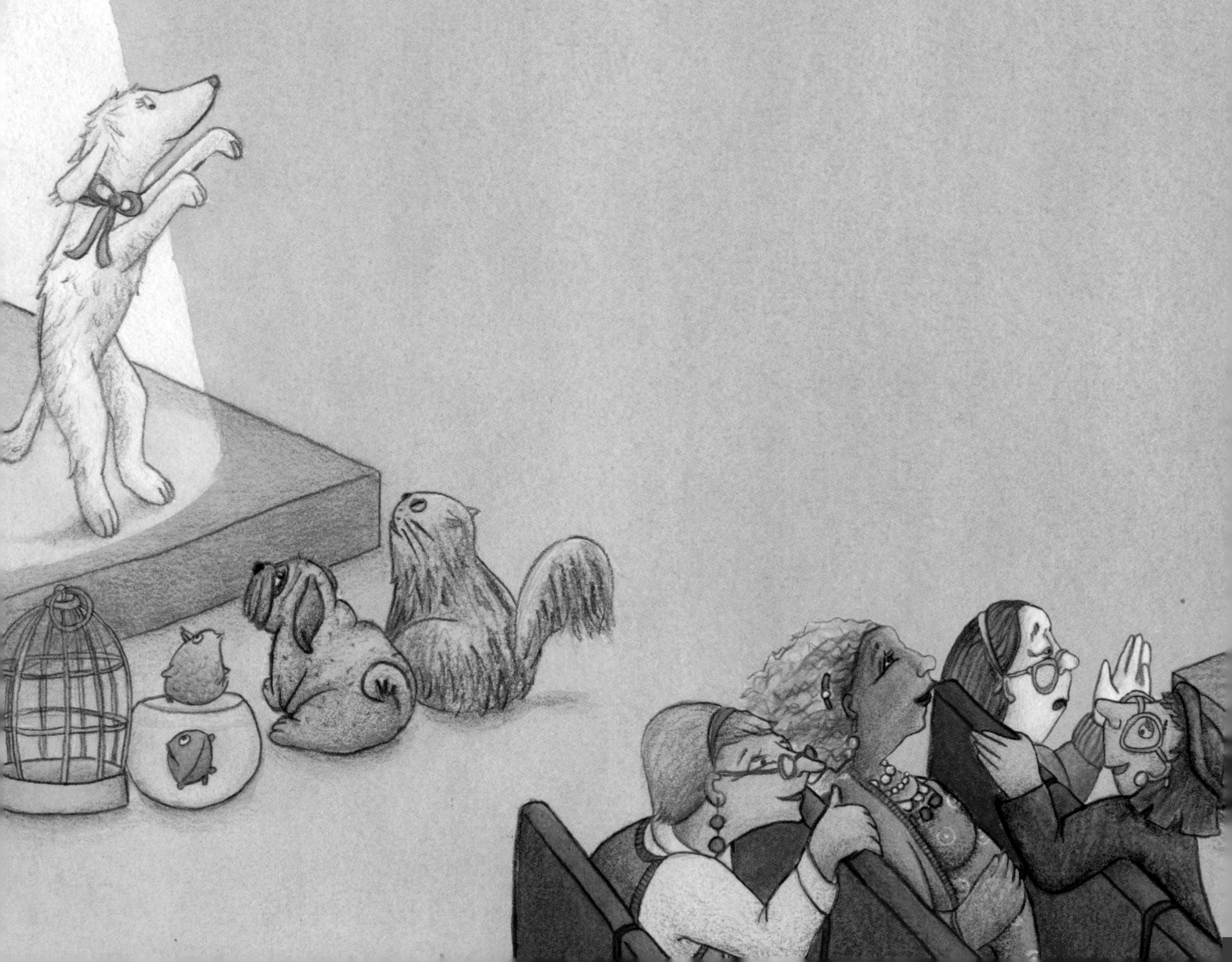

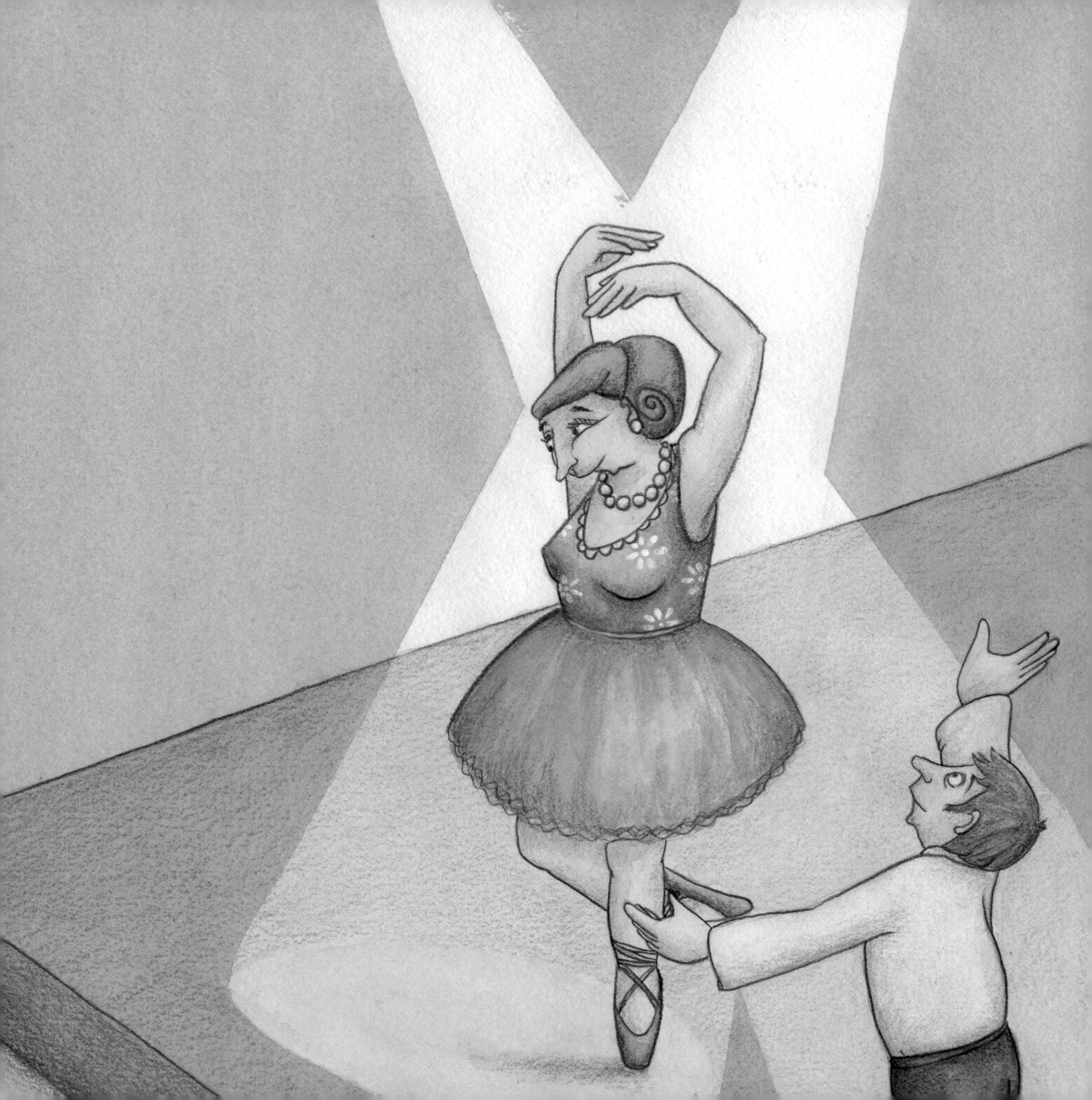

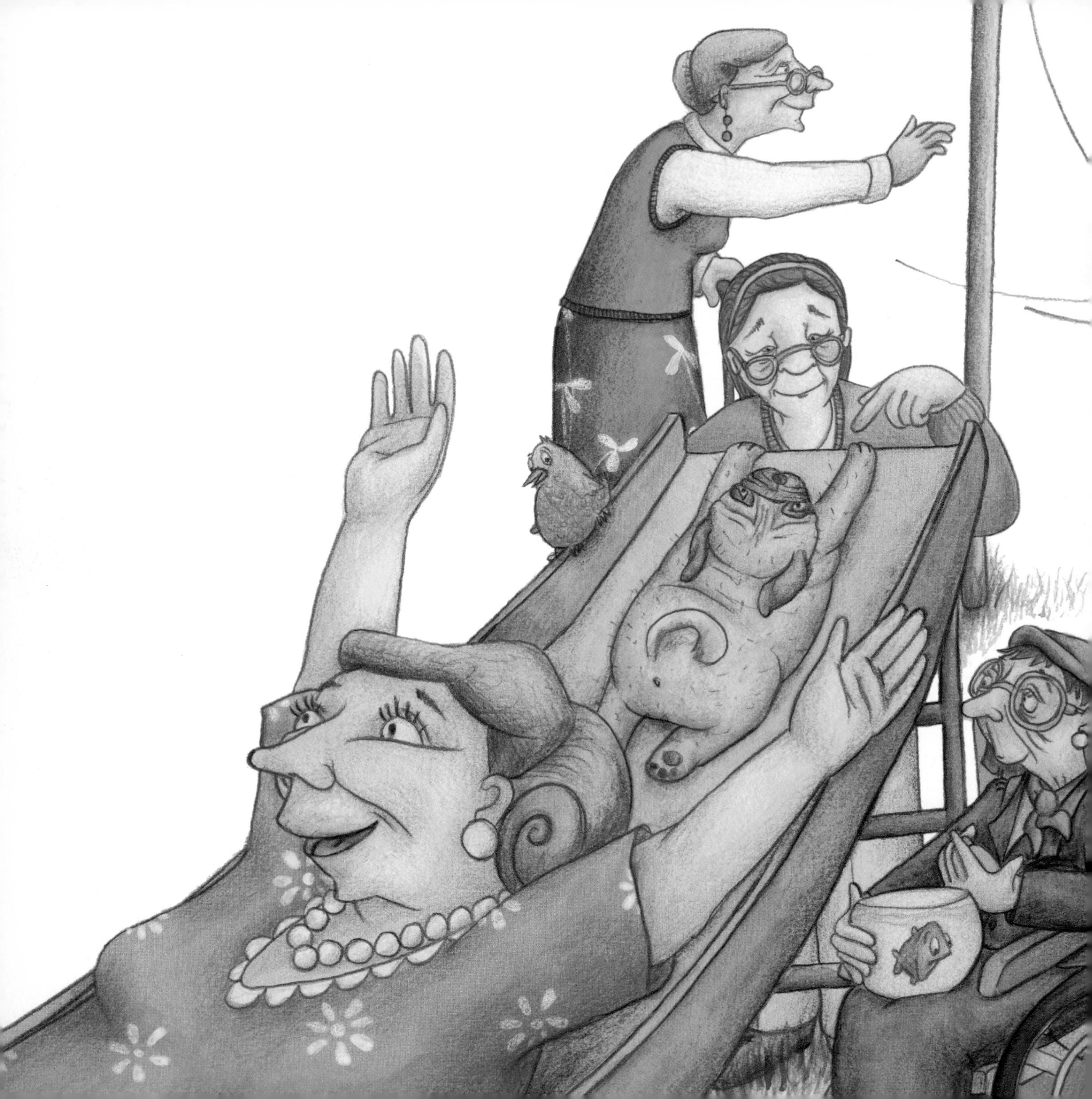

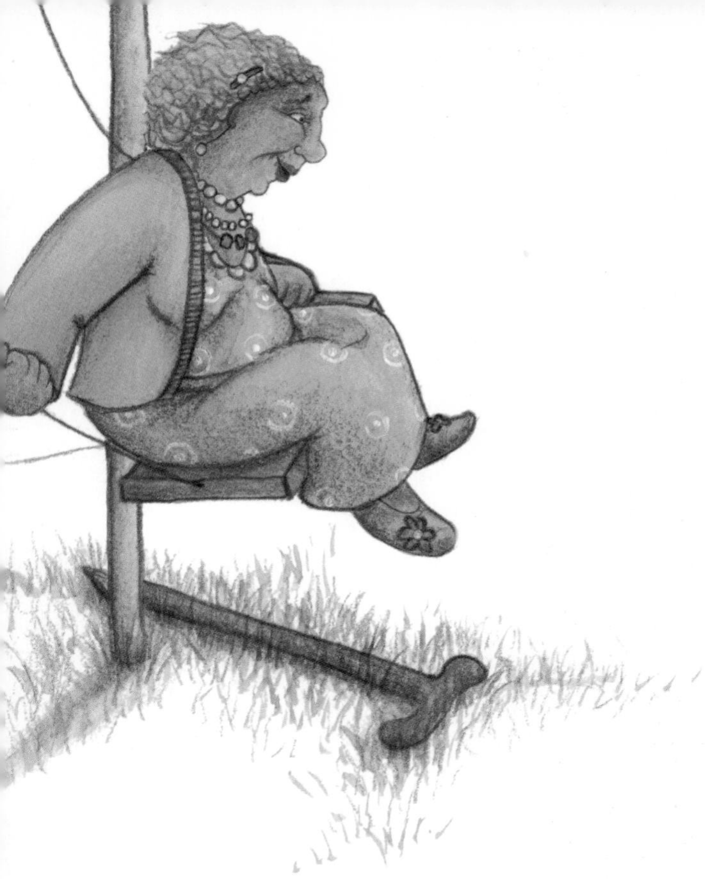

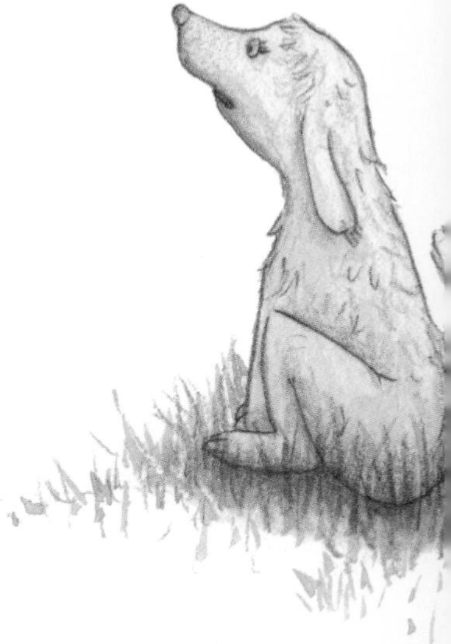

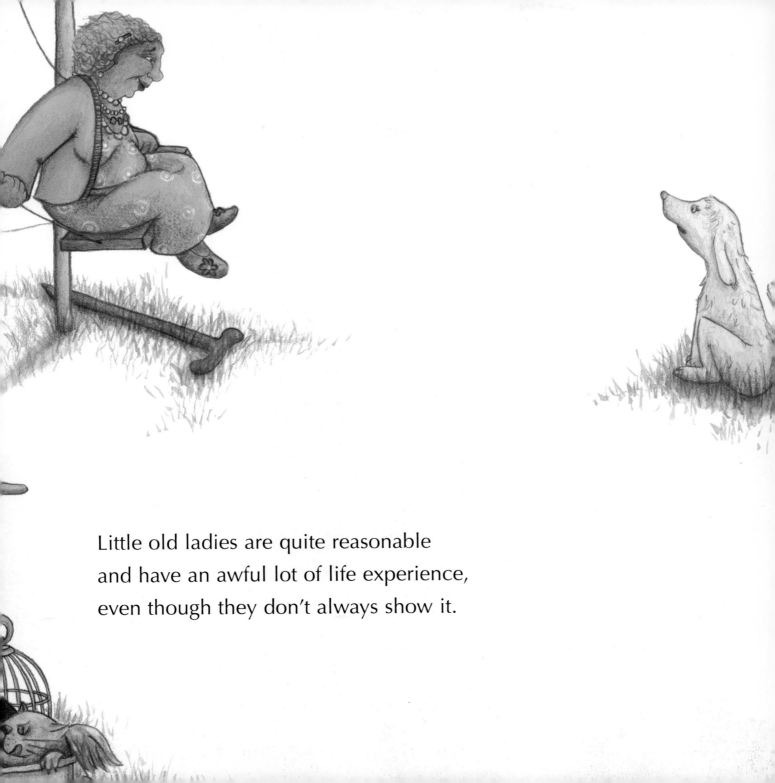

Little old ladies are quite reasonable
and have an awful lot of life experience,
even though they don't always show it.

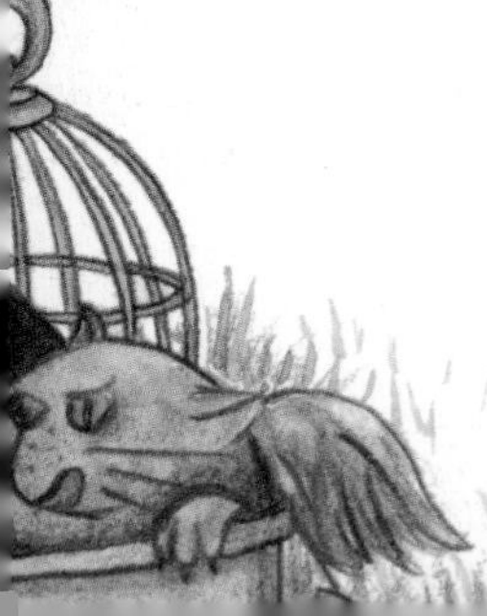

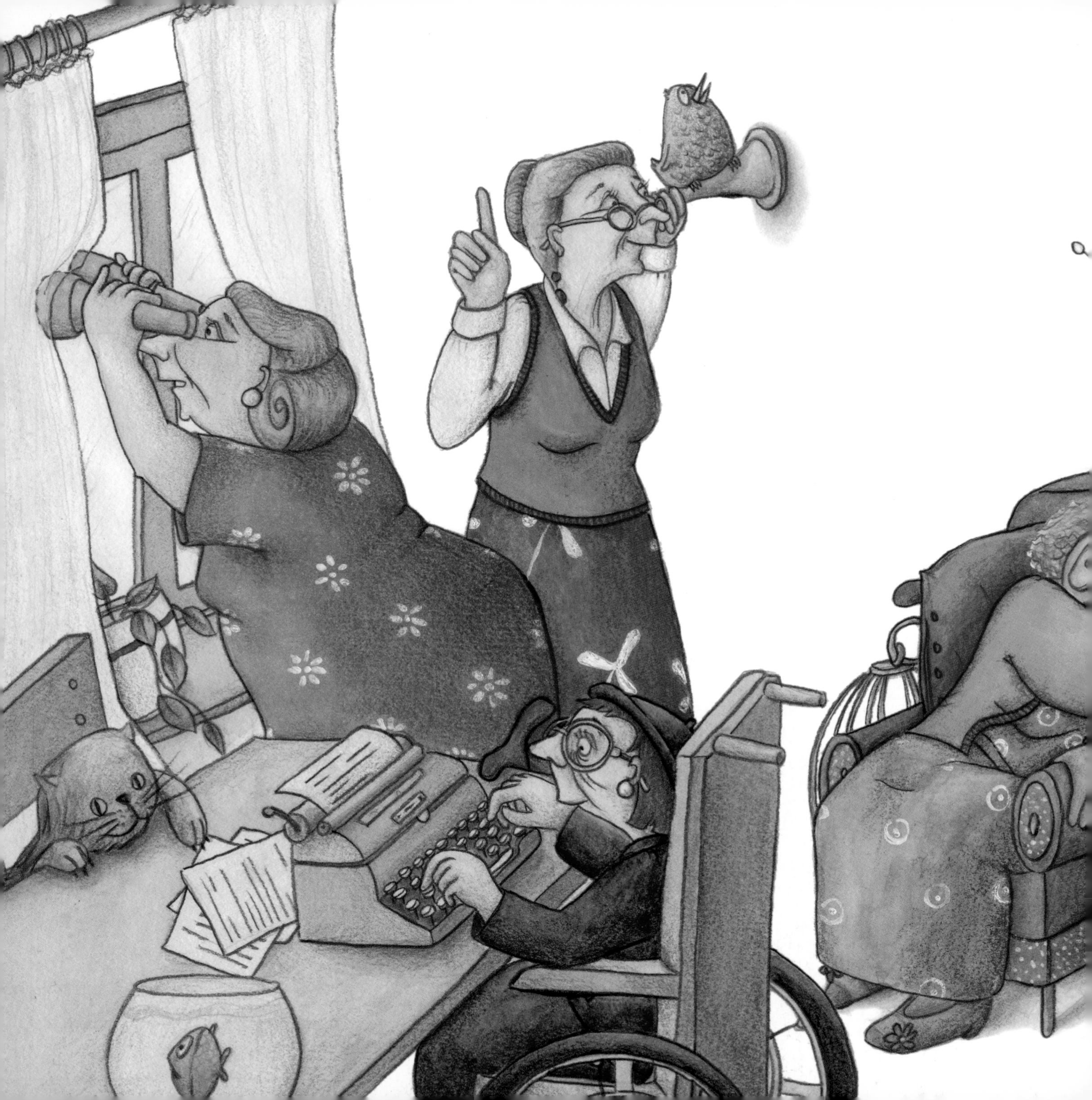

Little old ladies always seem to know exactly what's going on.
Nothing gets past them and they know all the tricks.

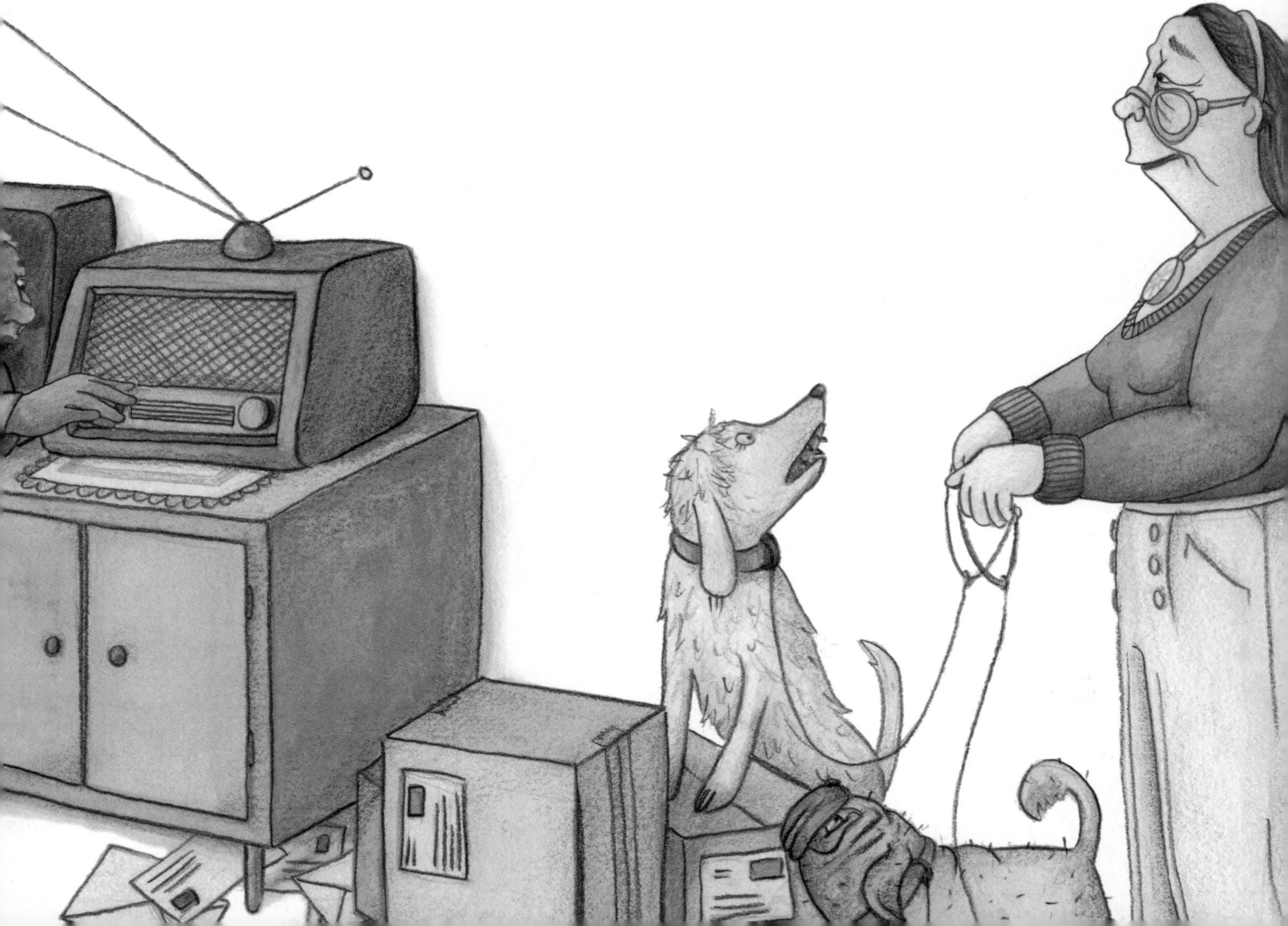

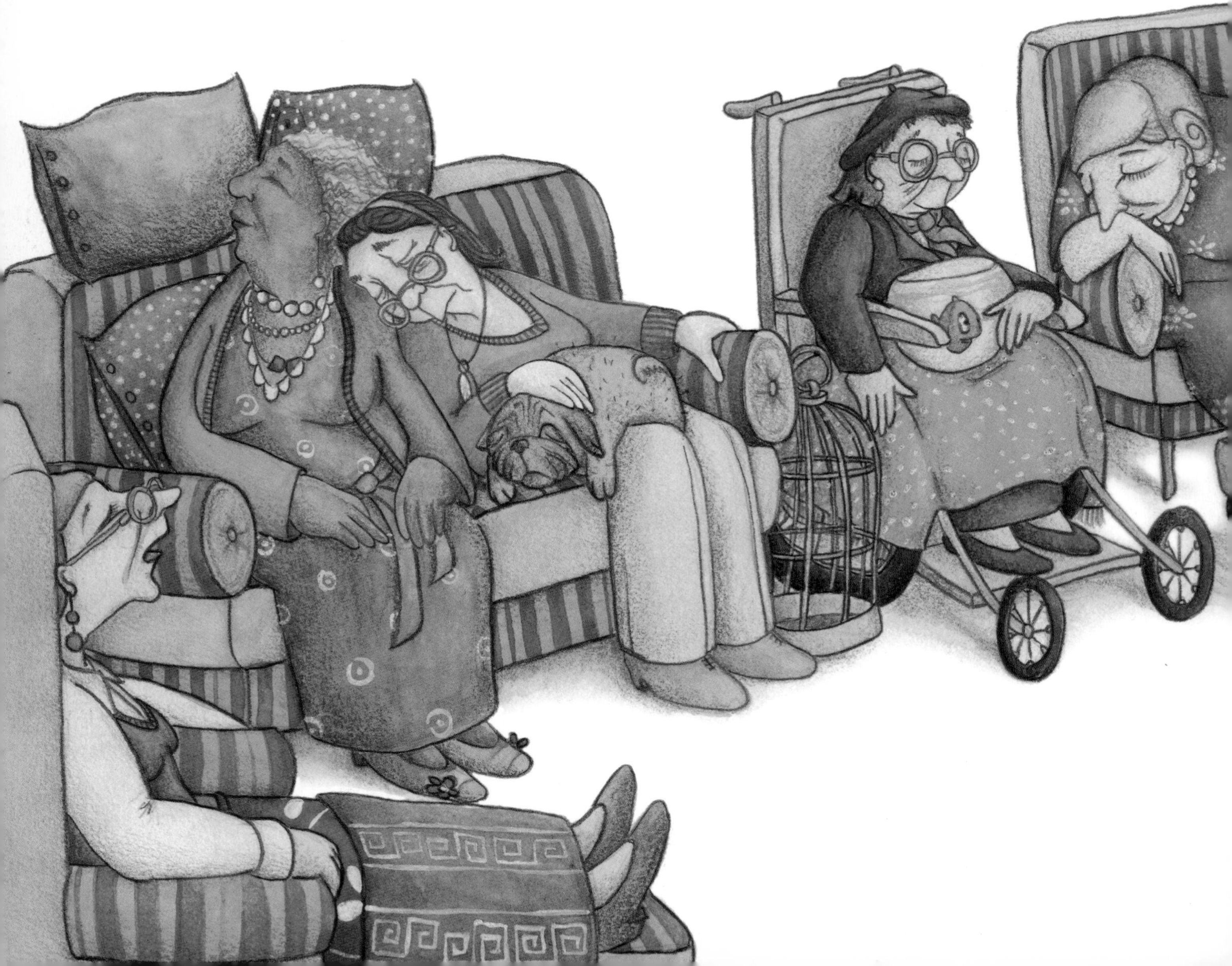

Little old ladies often don't sleep well at night,
but they make up for it during the day.

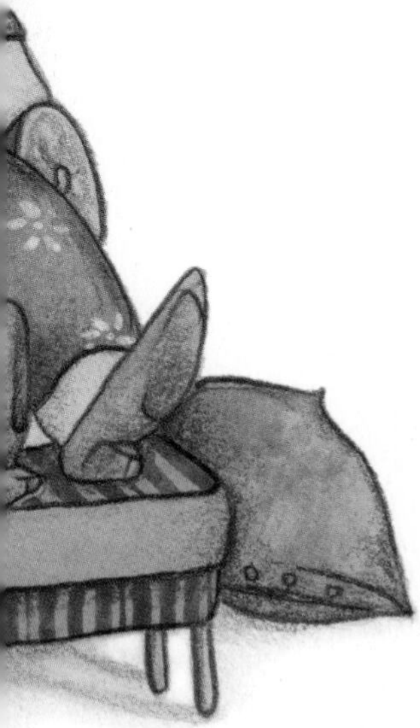

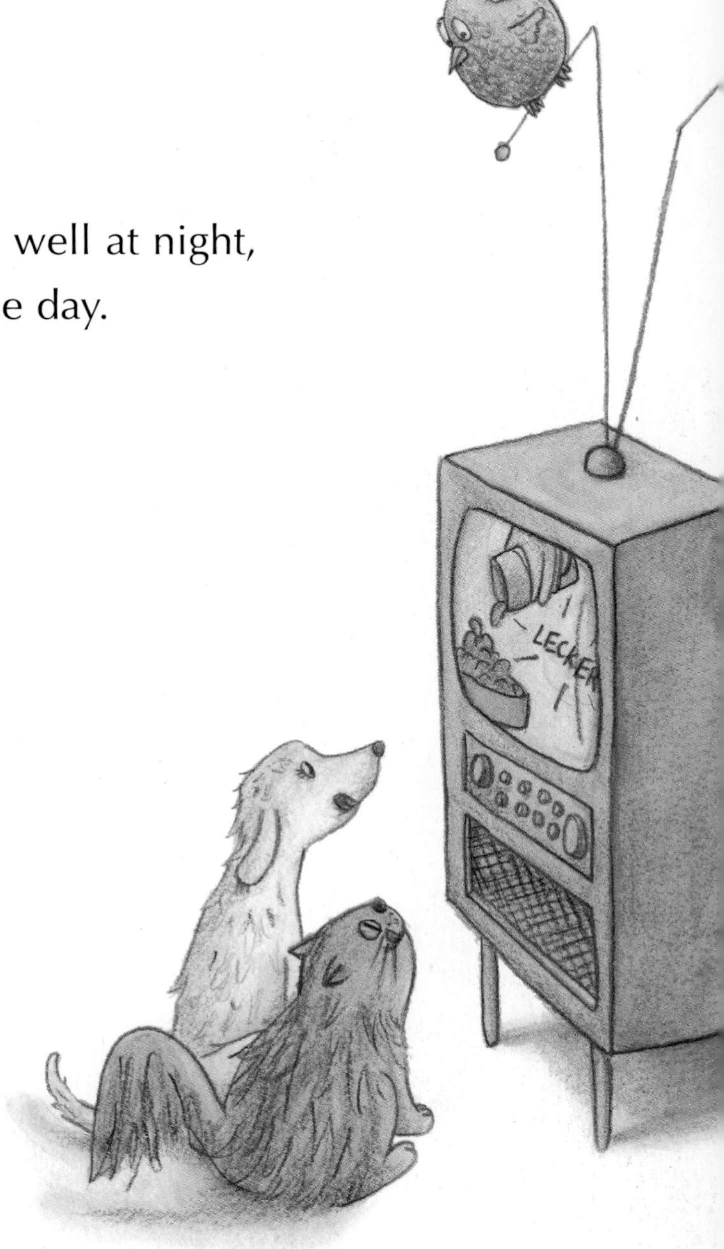
LECKER

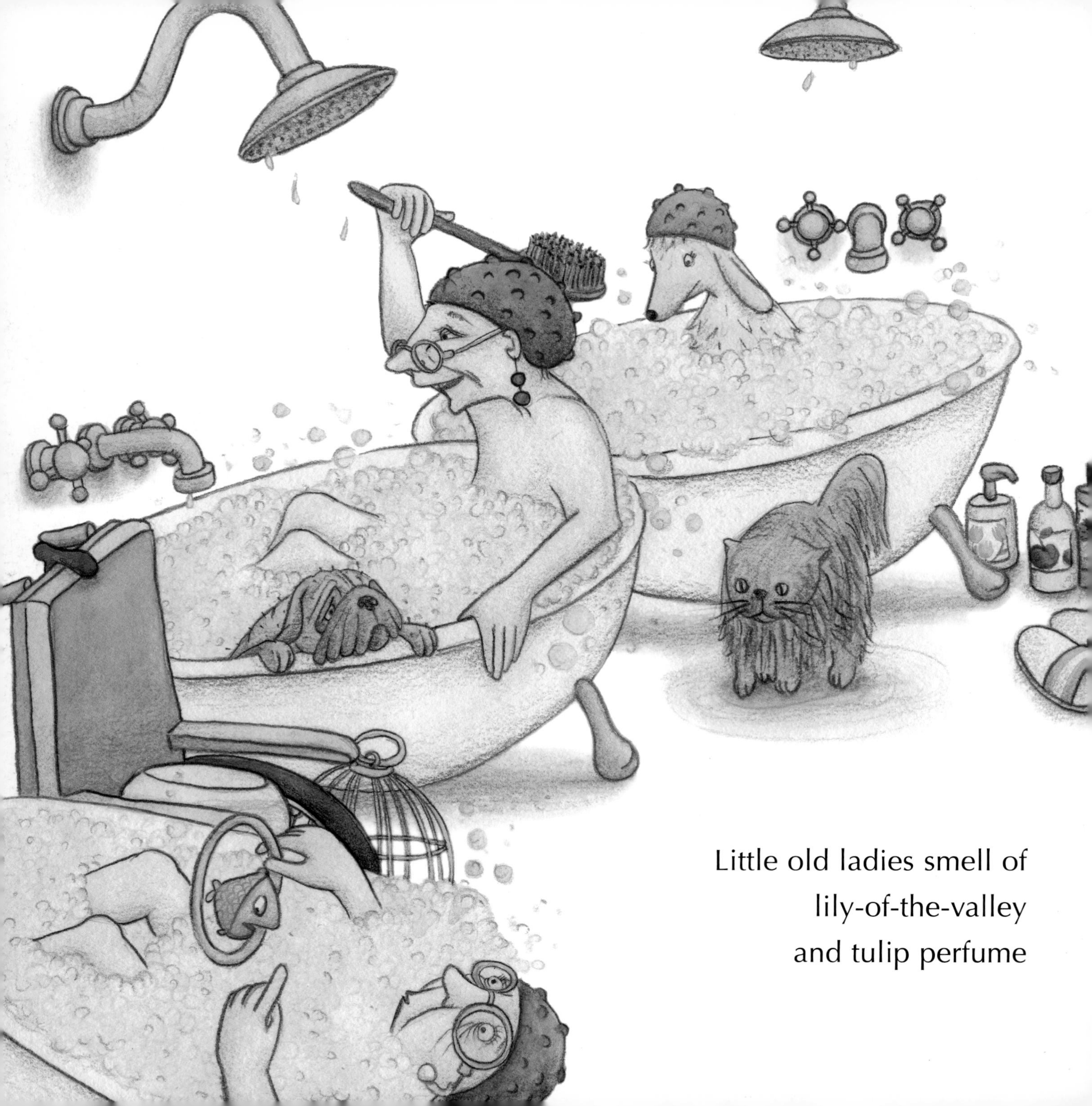

Little old ladies smell of
lily-of-the-valley
and tulip perfume

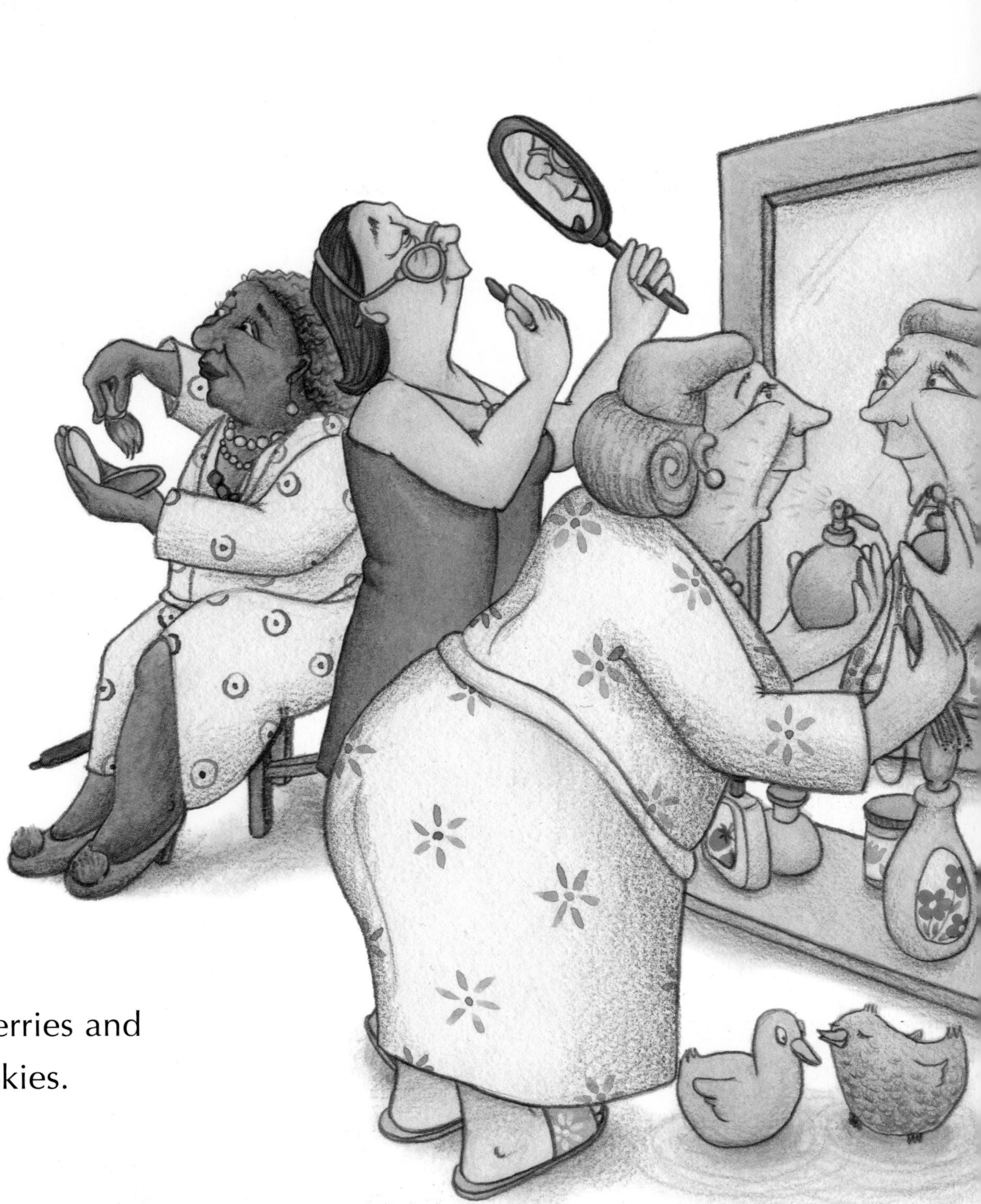

and of strawberries and
chocolate cookies.

Little old ladies love to dress up quite chic, of course,
and then they go dancing till the crack of dawn.

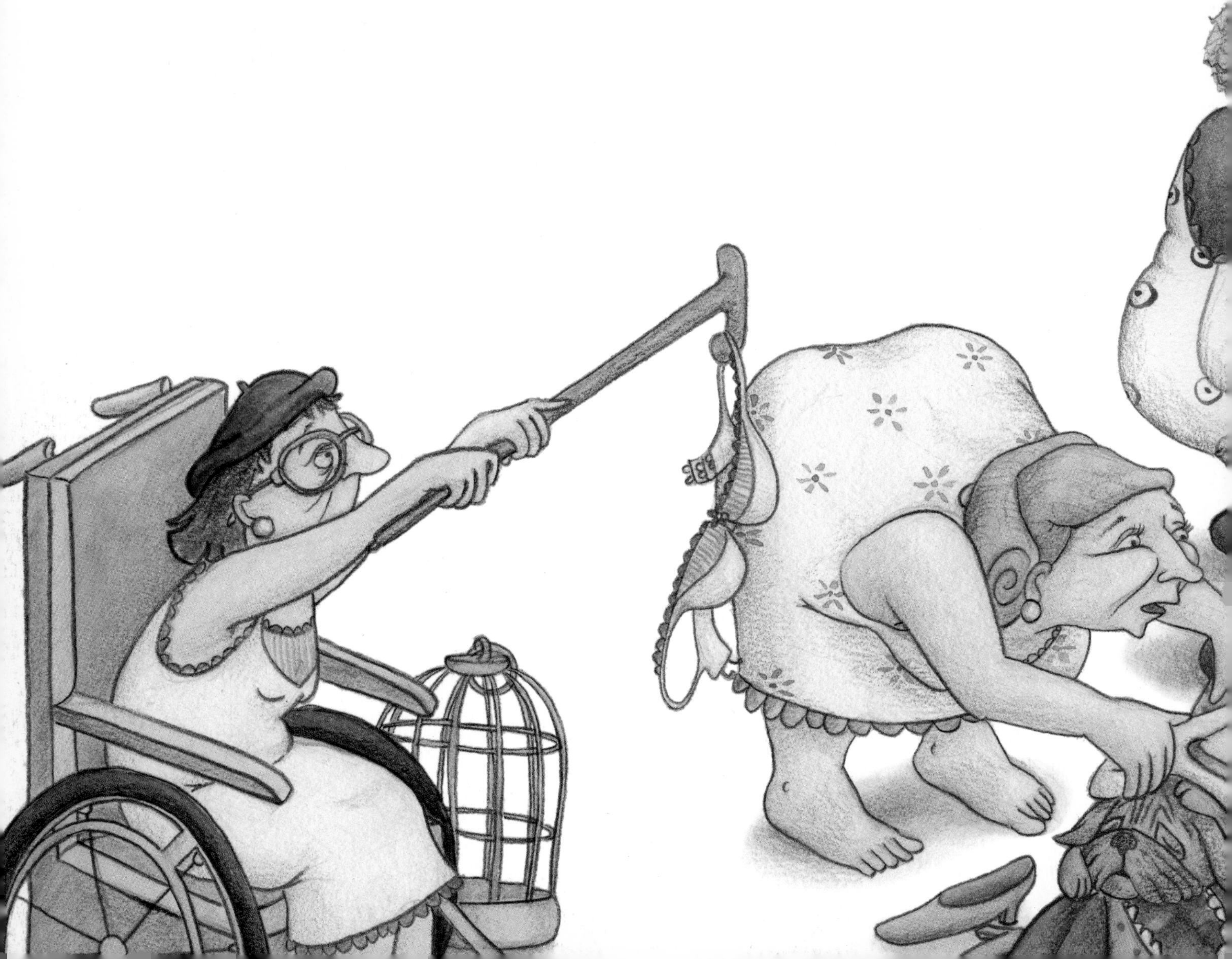

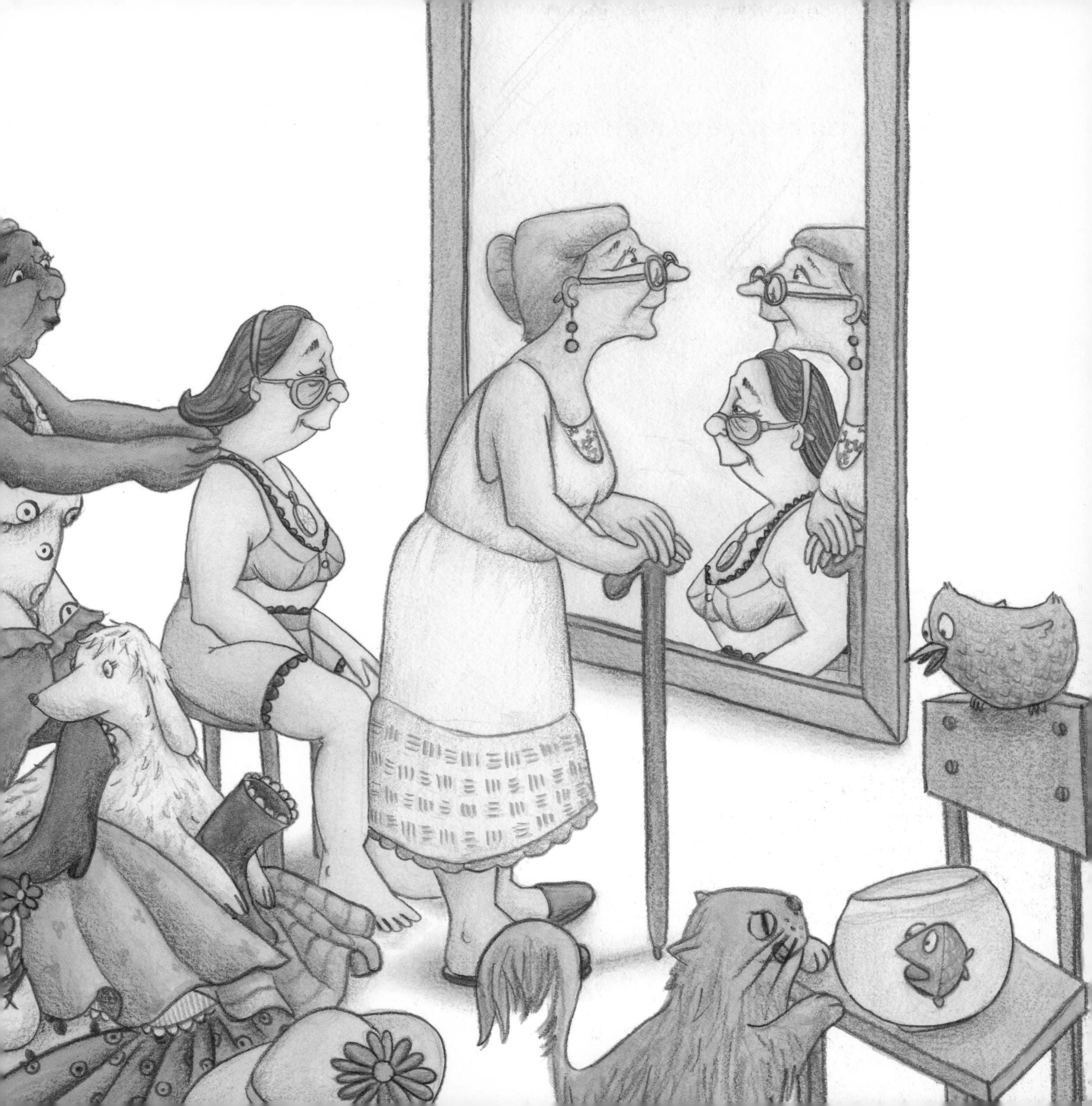

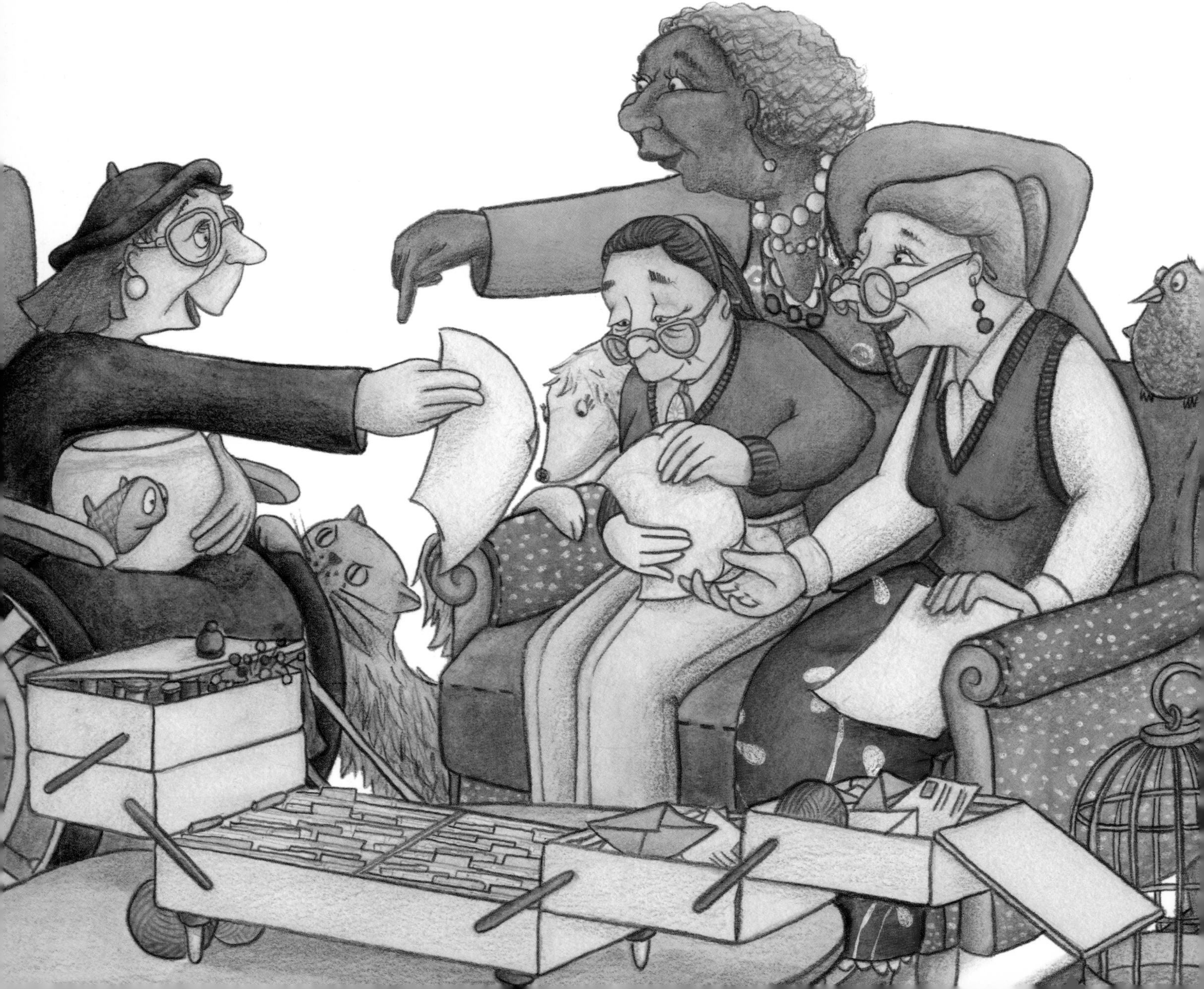

Little old ladies often have secret admirers.

But don't tell anyone, it's quite a secret, you see.

Little old ladies love outings in the country,
especially with all of their friends.
Little old ladies love having company.

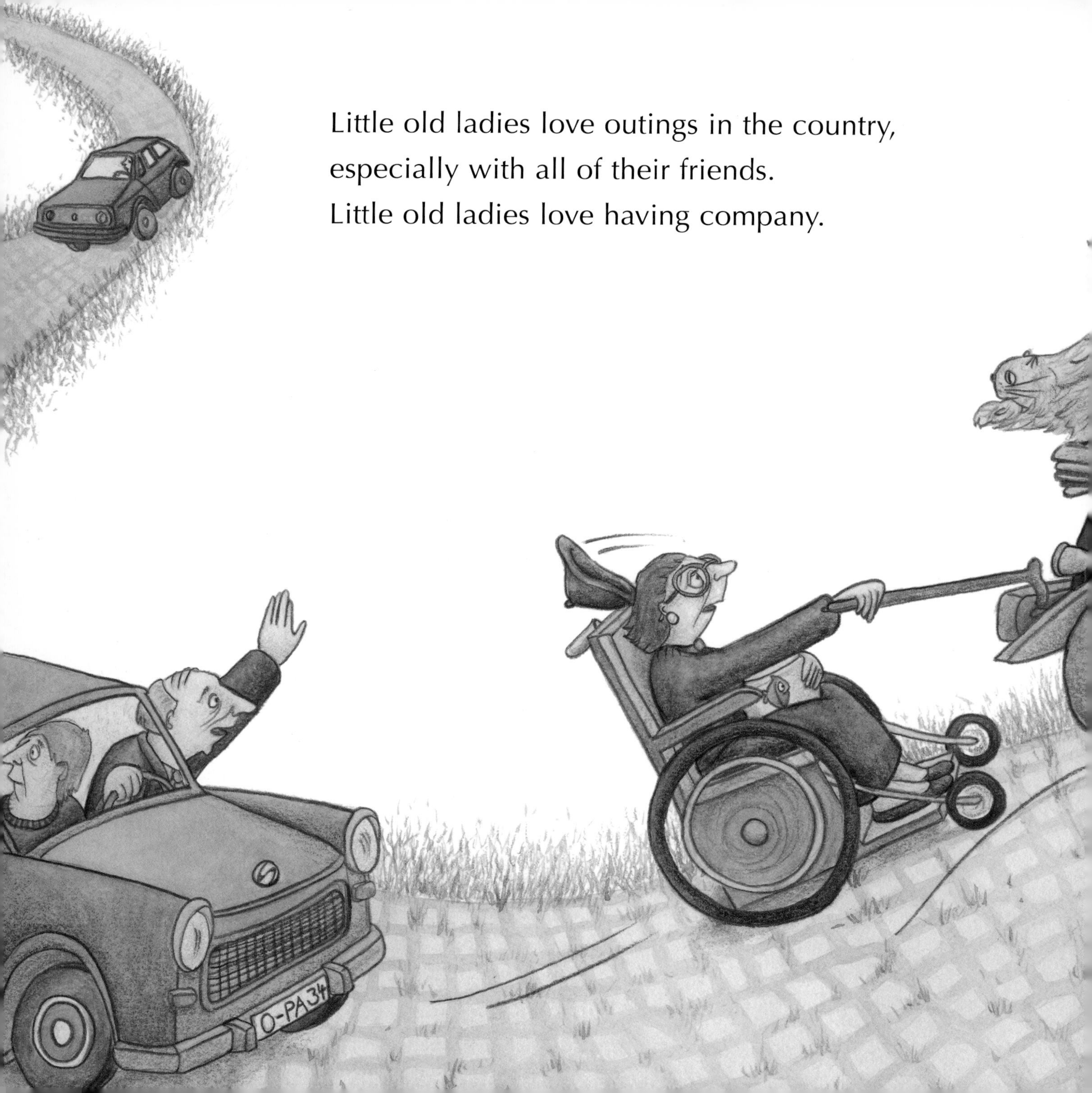
O-PA34

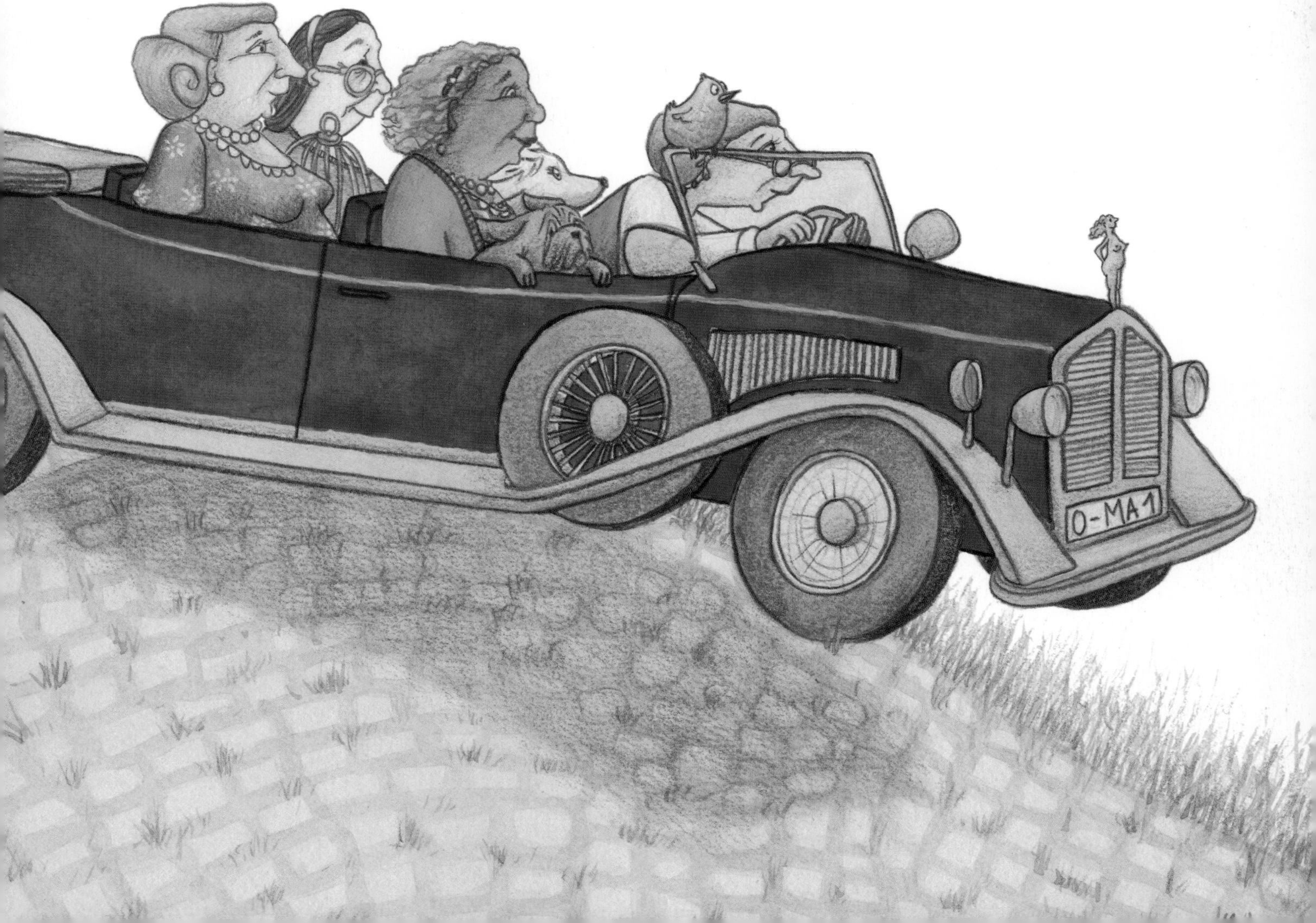
O-MA 1

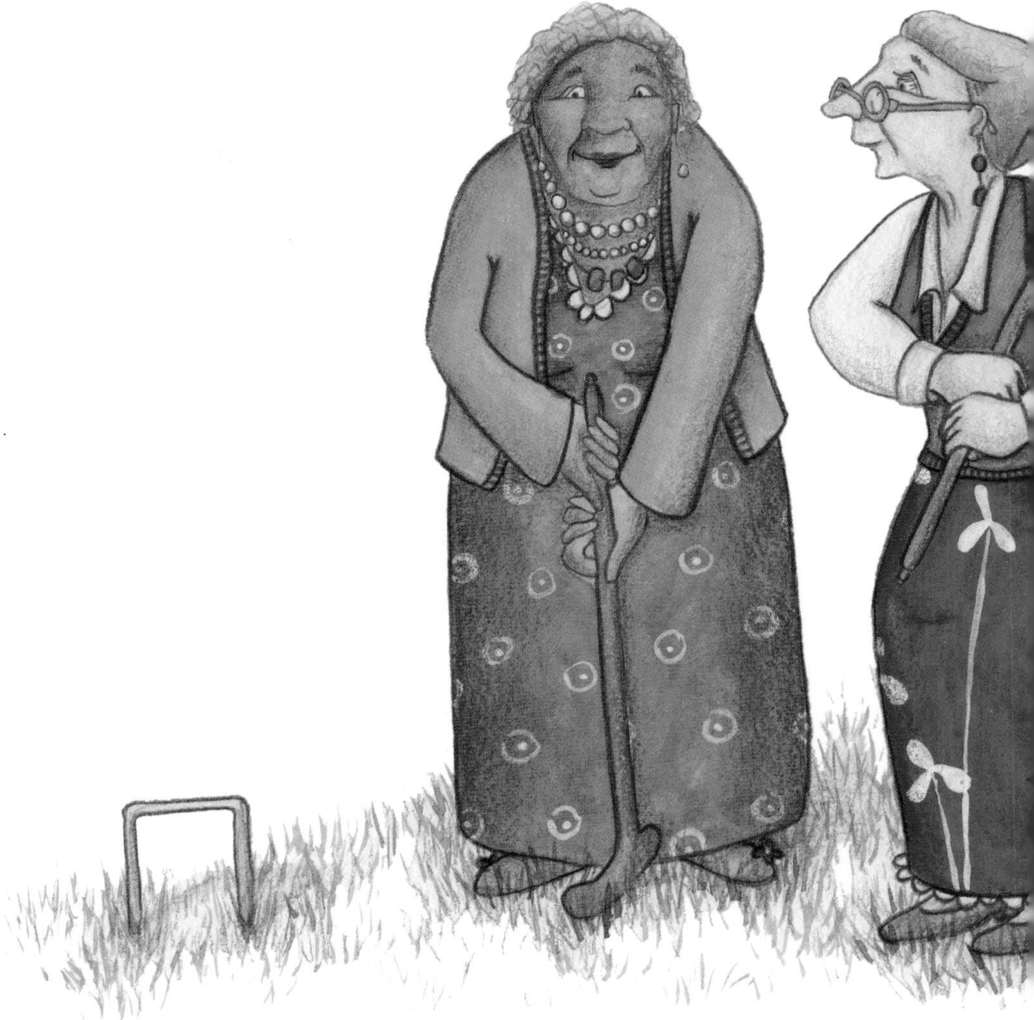

Little old ladies have a great deal of leisure time because they don't have to go to school anymore or go out and earn a living.

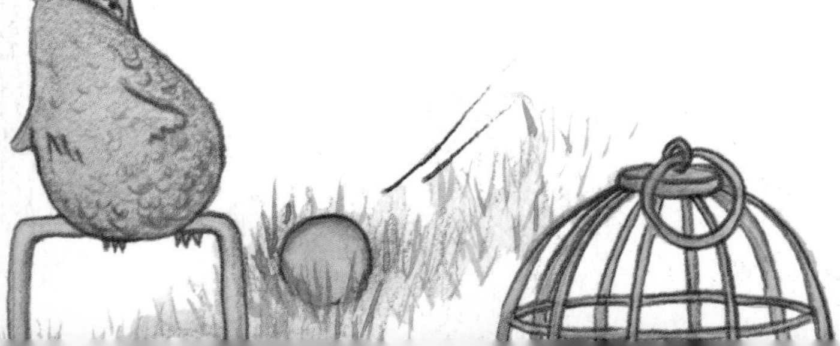

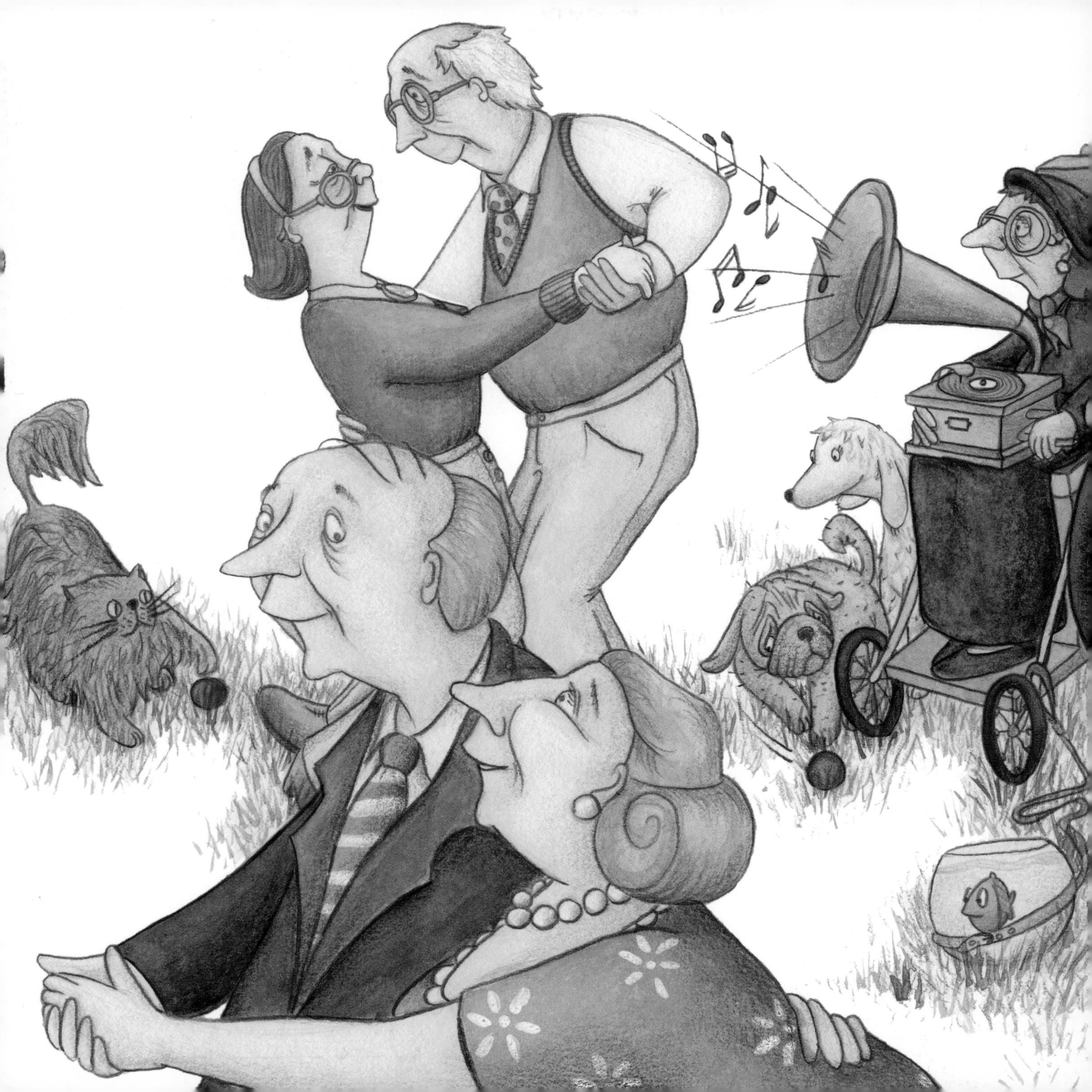

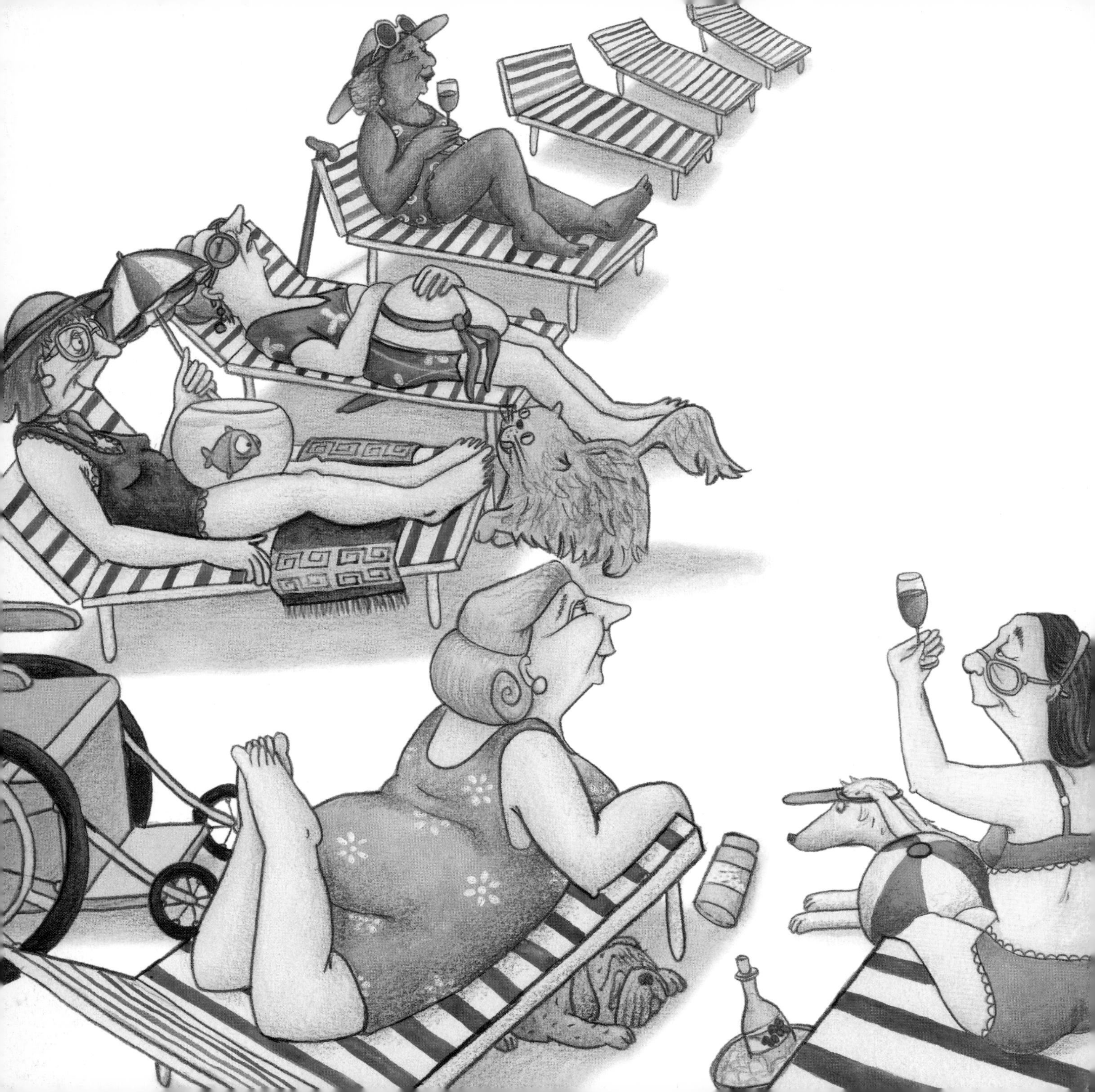

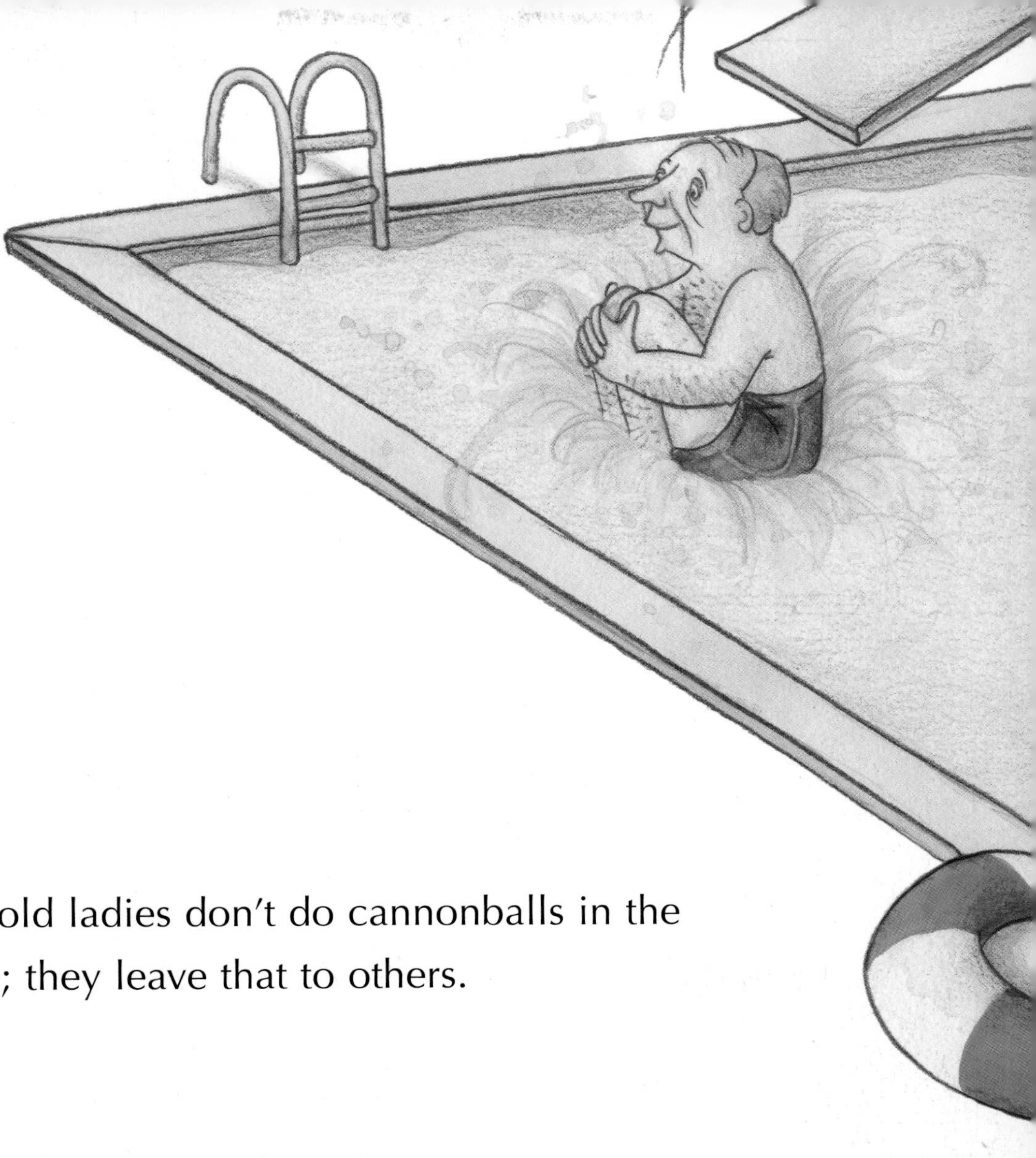

Unfortunately, little old ladies don’t do cannonballs in the pool much anymore; they leave that to others.

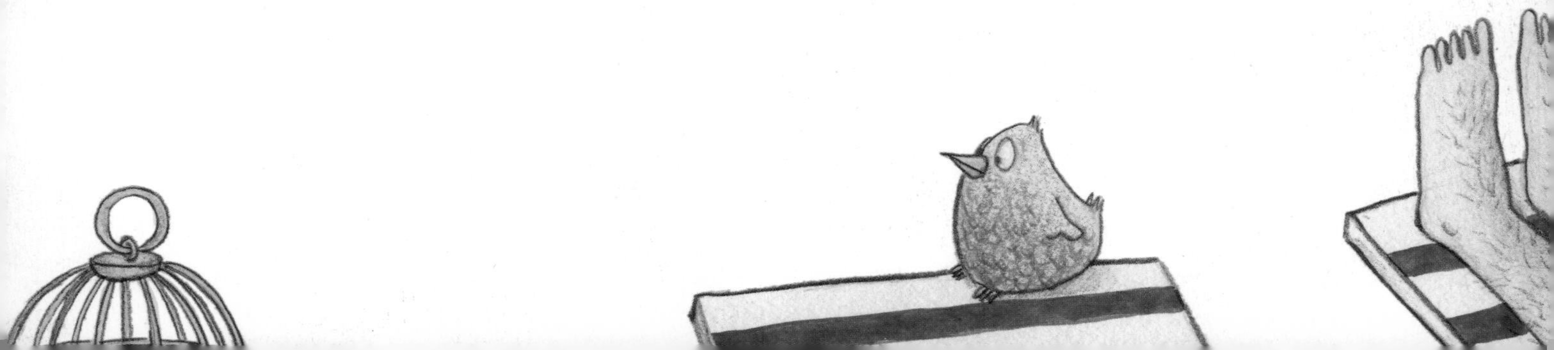

Little old ladies are always on time, when they meet for coffee and they never miss an opportunity to celebrate…anything! Who knows when they'll get the chance again!

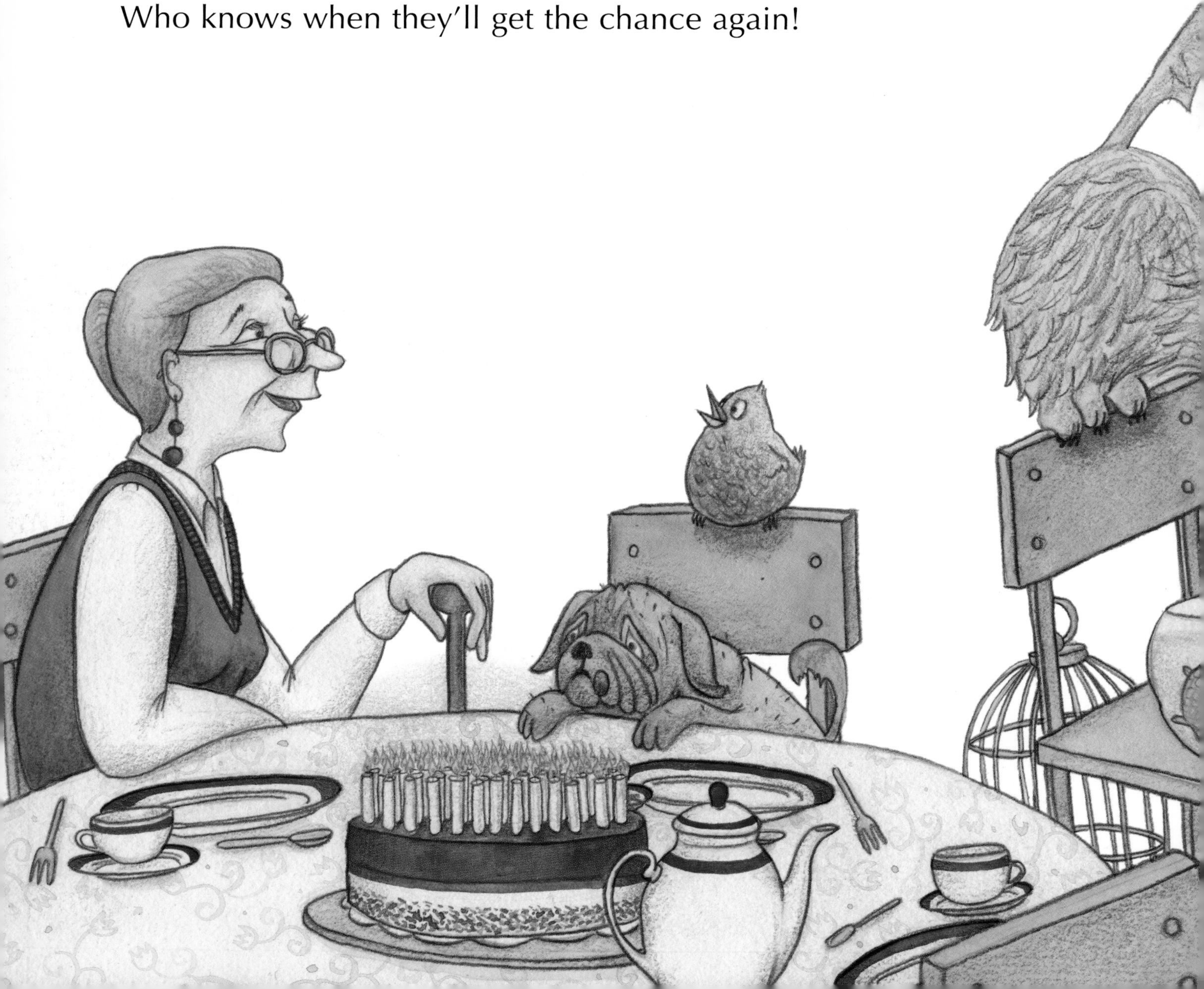

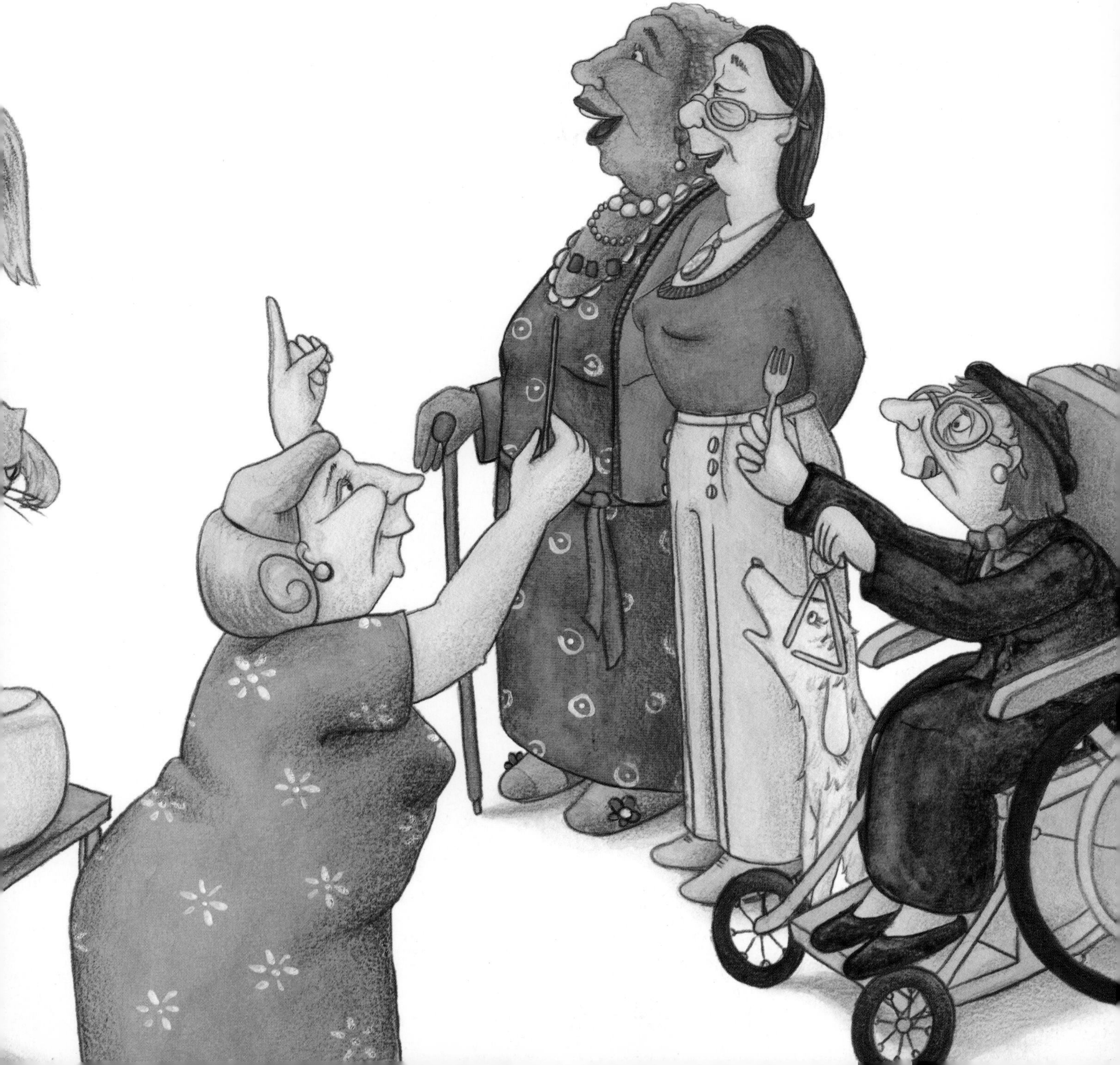

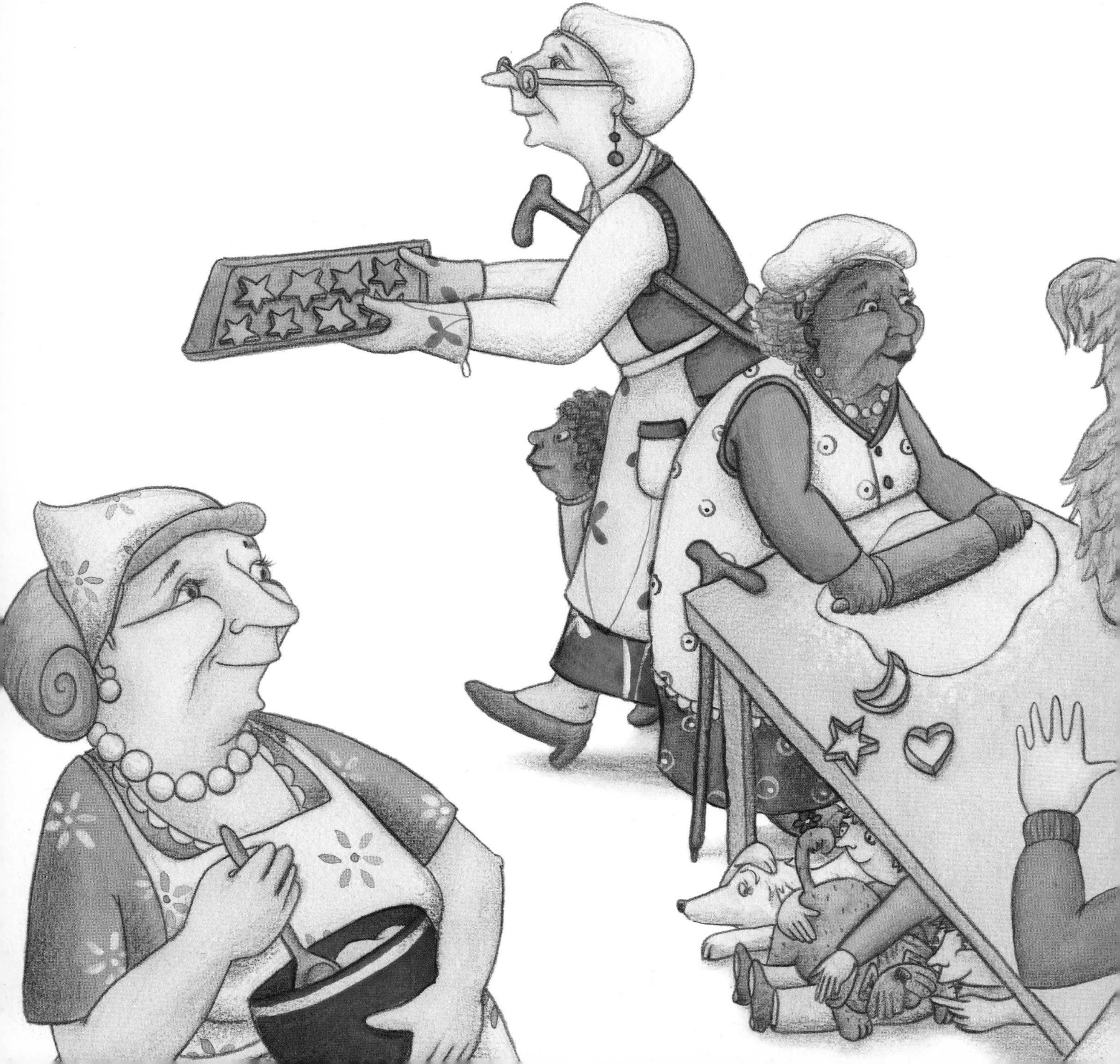

Little old ladies are brilliant at making cakes and cookies. They can whip up something wonderful just like magic when people come to visit.

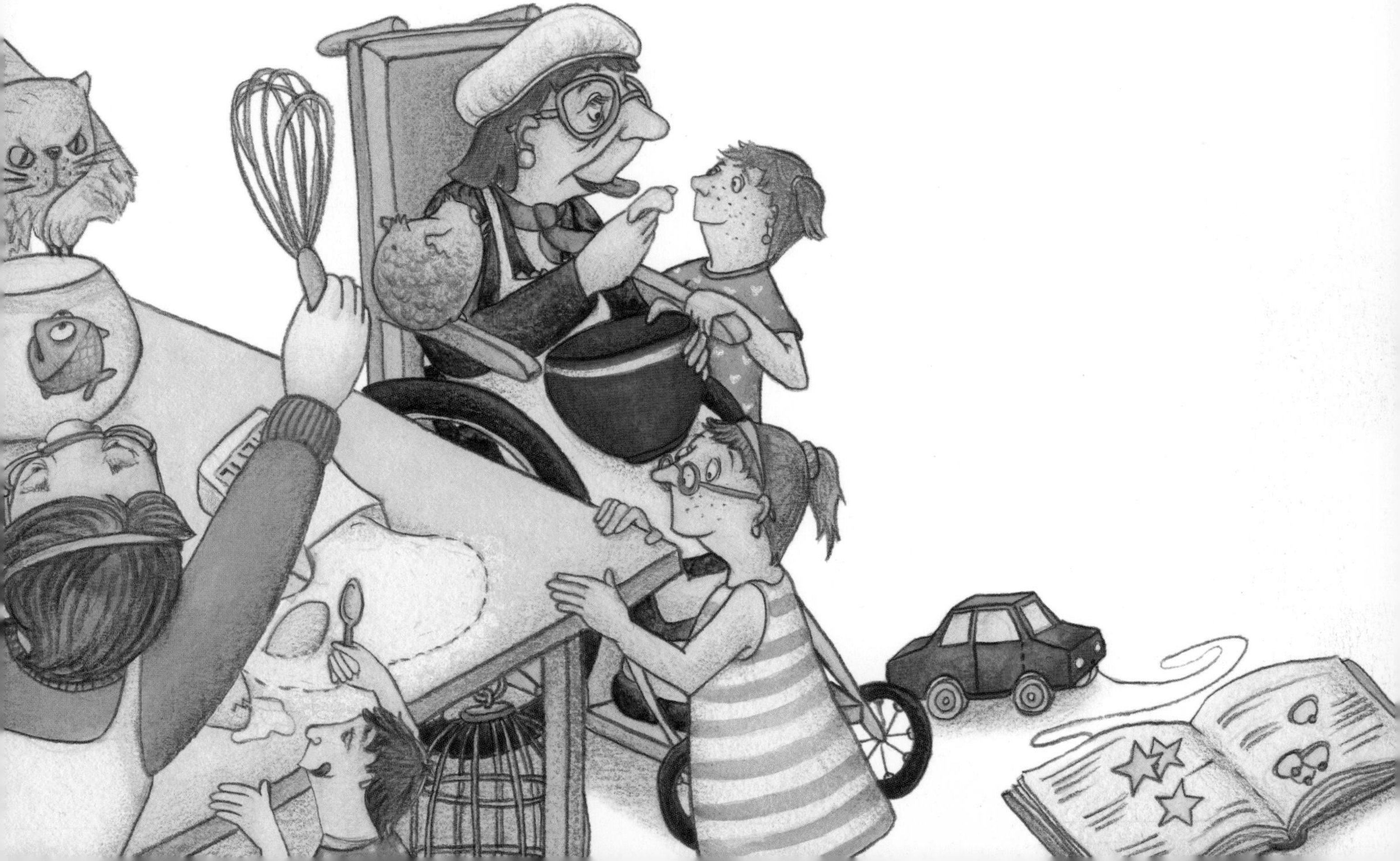

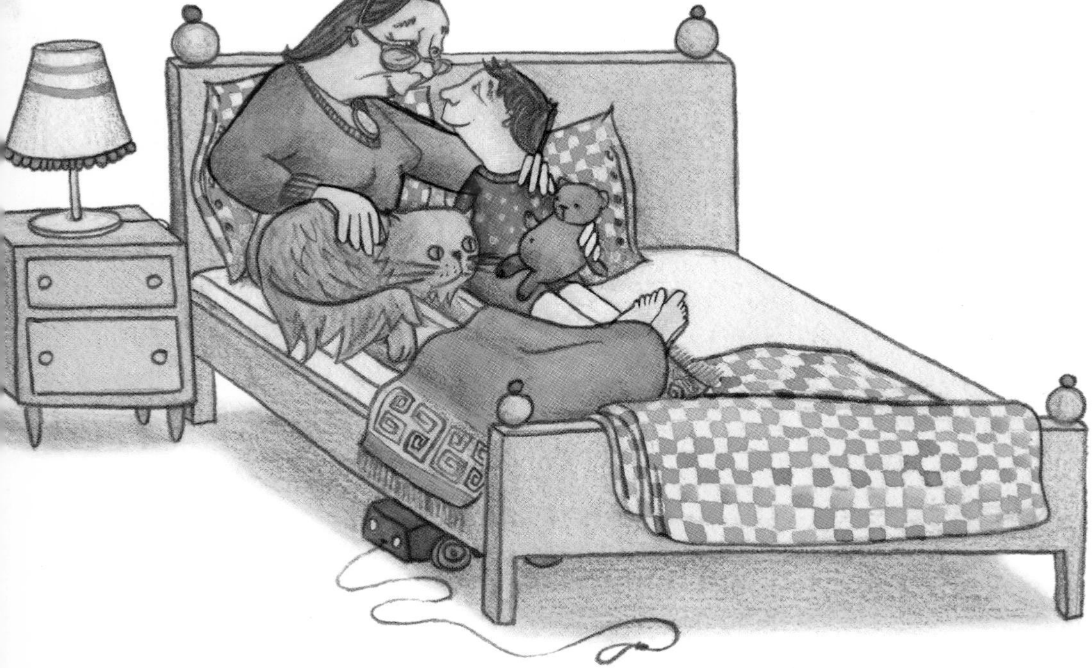

Little old ladies are like books of fairy tales–
they're full of stories all about the olden days.

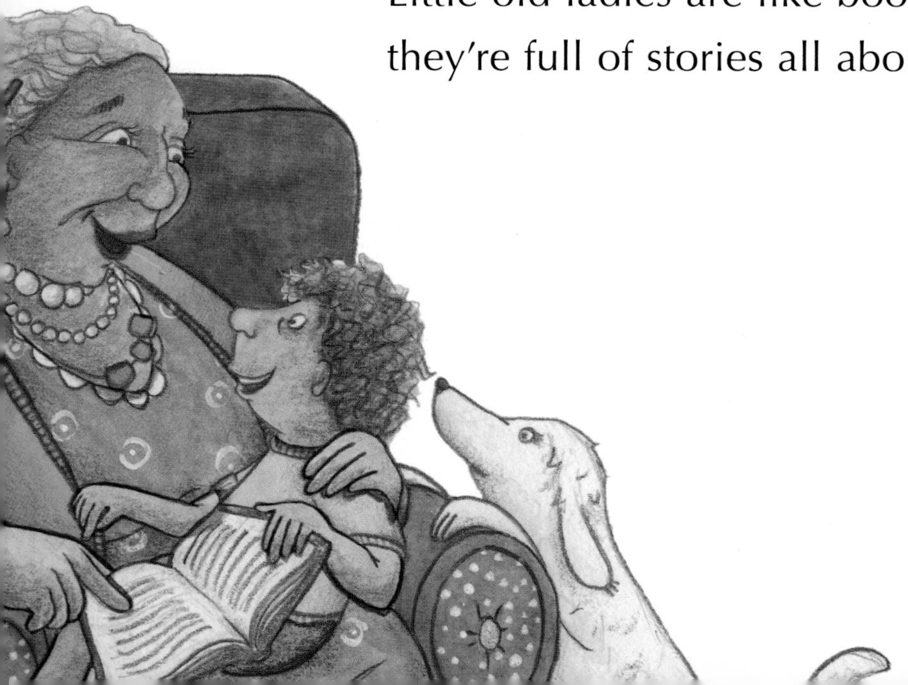

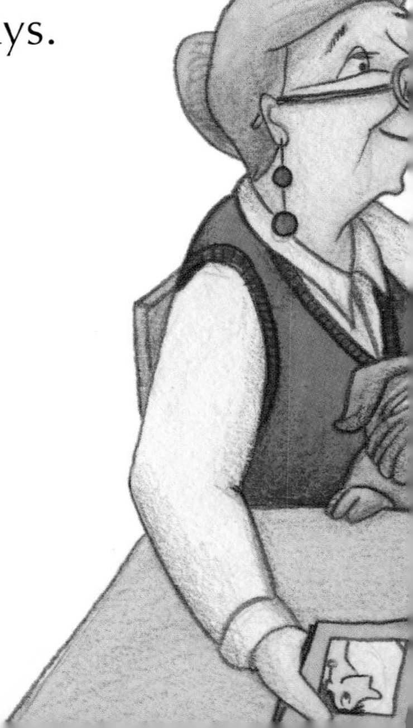

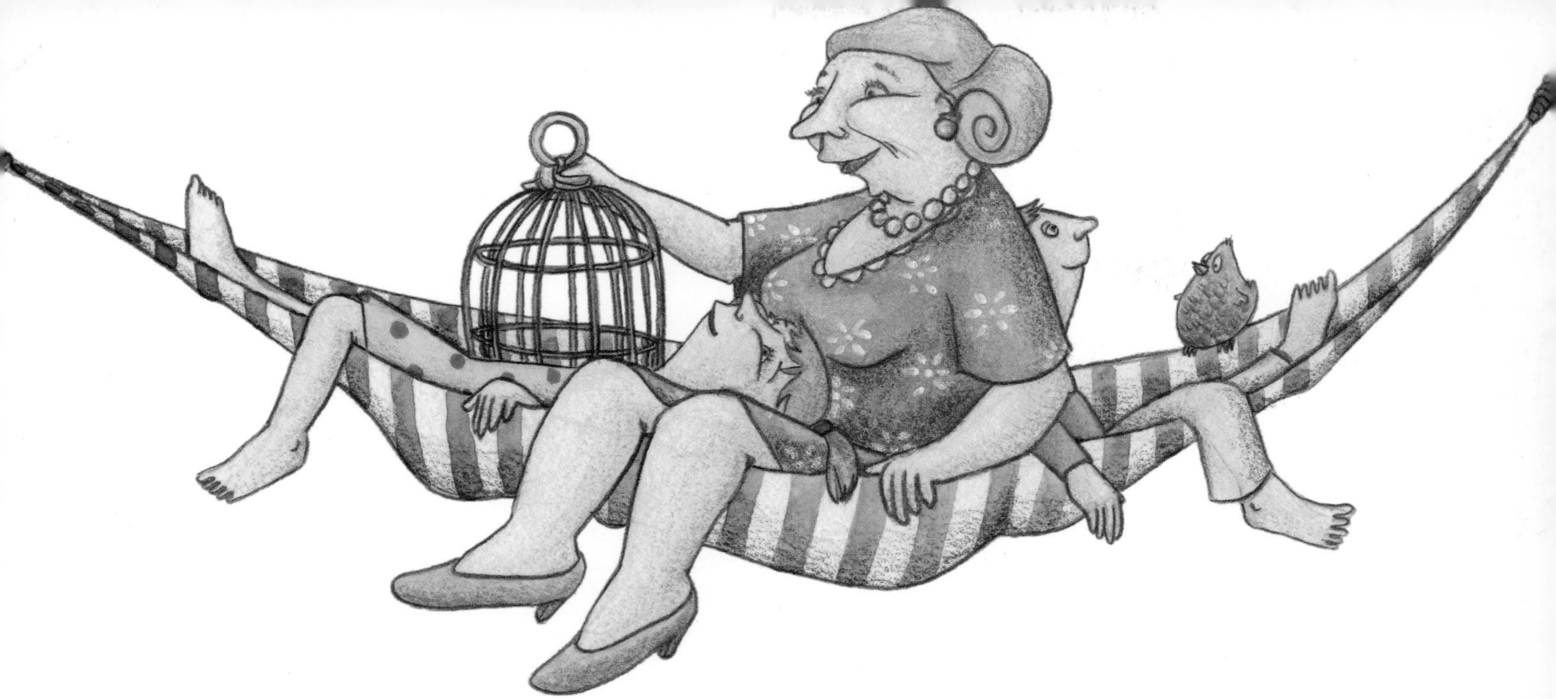

Little old ladies can tell us so much.
We only need to listen.

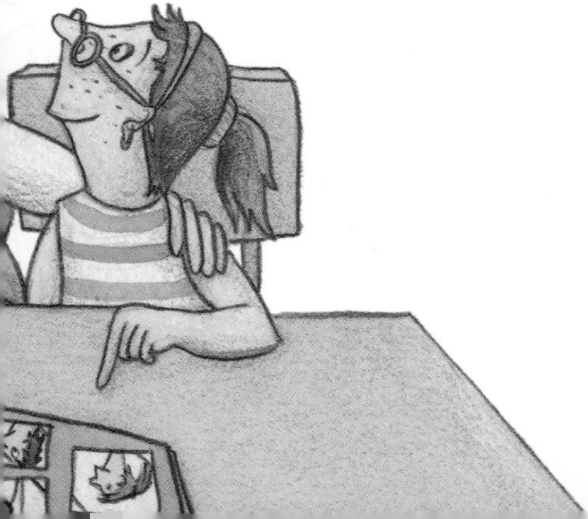

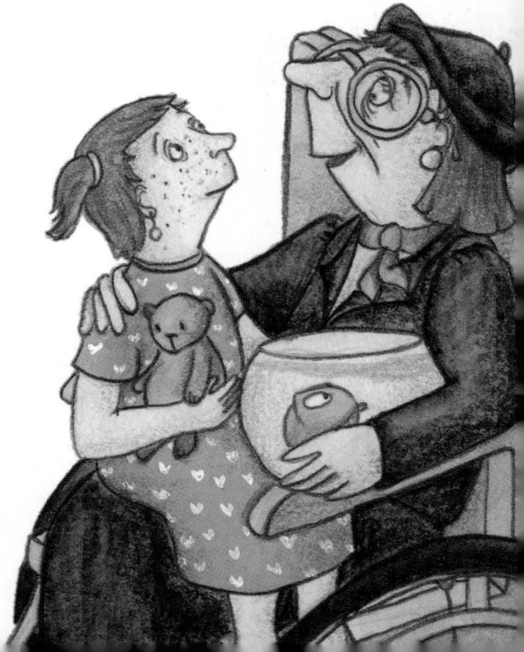

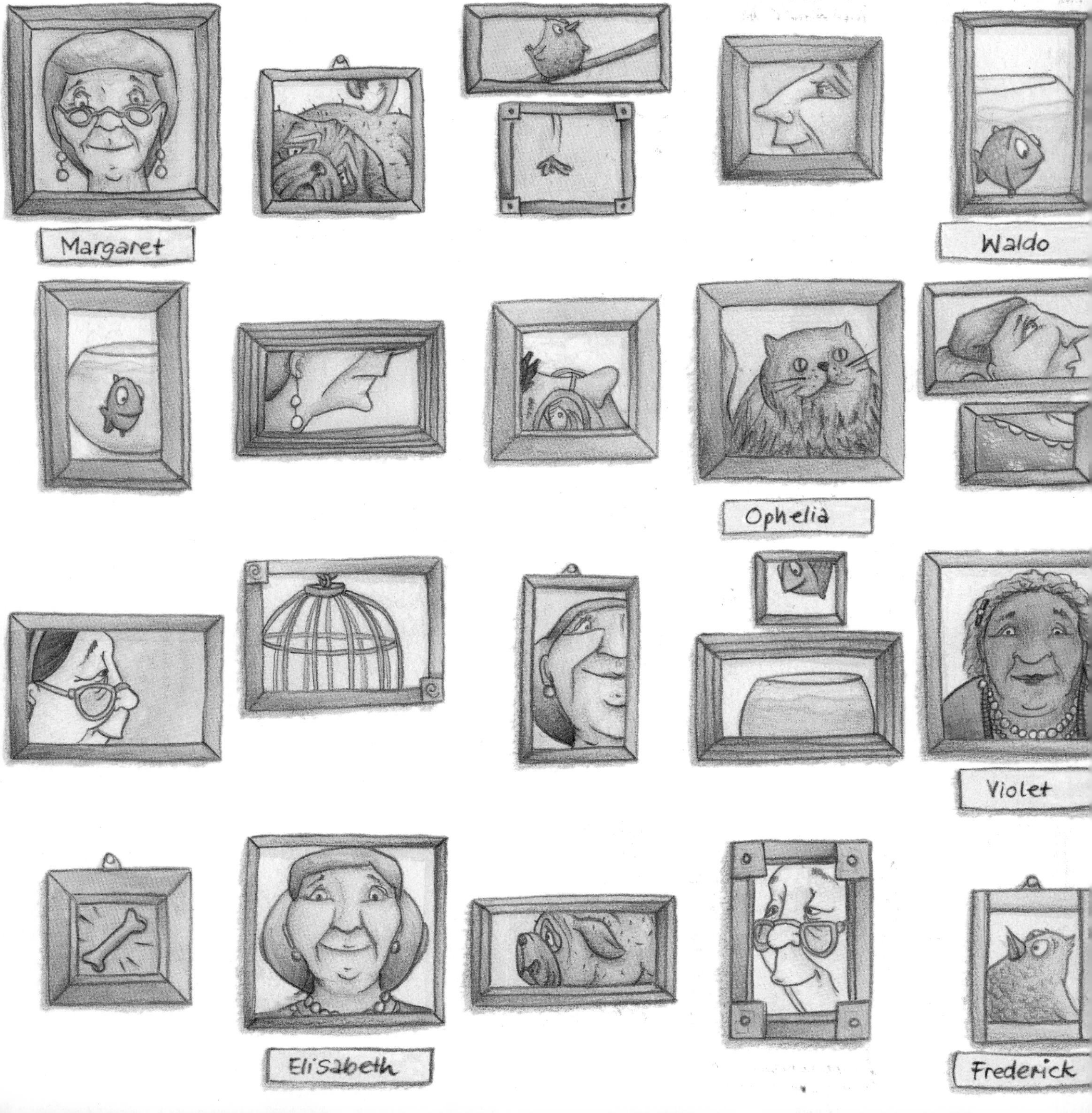
Margaret
Waldo
Ophelia
Violet
Elisabeth
Frederick